TO AUTUMN, WITH LOVE

THE SEASONS OF BELLE SERIES: BOOK 2

MICHELLE MONTEBELLO

Michelle Montebello is an Australian author and British English spelling is used in this novel.

Editing by Lynne Stringer and Marcia Batton
Cover design by Kris Dallas Designs.

ISBN: 978-0-6452296-5-3

To my mother.
With love always.

BLURB

A year on from Paris and Belle Hamilton is still searching for solace after all that she's lost.

When her father falls gravely ill, an astonishing truth is revealed, causing her to question everything she knew about herself.

Searching for answers, she travels to Scotland with her partner, Andre, and her friend, Riley, determined to discover her lost past.

Amidst the raw beauty of the Highlands and the stunning Scottish coastlines, Belle pursues a man who holds the key to it all. But finding him is not easy, as he eludes her, leaving a trail of questions behind.

Will Scotland reveal what Belle desperately seeks, or has the past been lost forever to the seasons?

BLURB

'As summer into autumn slips,
And yet we sooner say,
"The summer" than "the autumn",
Lest we turn the sun away.
~ Emily Dickinson

ONE

It was a cool night, the moon balancing in a black sky, as Belle stood outside the restaurant with her colleagues, watching the owner, Carlo, lock up. The dinner shift at The Olive Grove had been busy, dockets overwhelming the pass, her fingertips still tingling from the heat of the flames as she'd juggled multiple pans. Despite the packed dining room and endless orders, they'd still managed to close on time, and everyone was impatient for a nightcap.

'You're coming,' Carlo insisted, glancing at her from over his bulky shoulder, as he deadlocked the front door.

Belle braced herself for the heckling. 'Not tonight.'

'You never come out with us,' Stacy the head waitress whined, smearing a fresh coat of lipstick on her lips.

'Come on, Hamilton. One drink,' Kieran said. He was standing beside her, his chef's whites replaced with dark jeans and a collared shirt that defined his well-sculpted arms.

Belle glanced at her watch, then up at the partygoers surging along Argyle Street like a tidal wave. Friday night.

Hordes of people. *You can't see a gunman in a horde of people.* 'I'd better not. It's getting late.'

'It's not that late.' Kieran touched the small of her back, a hopeful look in his eyes. 'We'll just go for one and I'll walk you home afterwards.'

Belle shook her head apologetically. 'No, thanks. Maybe next time.' Someone behind him sniggered, but she ignored them and waved goodbye. 'Have fun. See you tomorrow.'

Kieran sighed with disappointment, then their voices faded as they turned and walked in the direction of Argyle Street, towards the crowds. She headed away from them, taking the quieter route to her house.

She knew her colleagues didn't understand why she refused to join them, why the thought of standing in a packed bar like a can of sardines made her heart race and her throat tighten. She'd never told them about Paris, and yet they always included her, no matter how often she turned them down—especially Kieran, who she worked with in the kitchen, and whom she'd long suspected had a crush on her.

She'd been a sous chef at The Olive Grove for the past year. After returning home from Paris, she'd discovered the job advertised on a local community Facebook page and had applied. Carlo and Kieran had interviewed her, impressed with her culinary experience in Rome, and had hired her on the spot.

It was one of many restaurants in town, tucked away just off the main street, and popular with the locals for the authentic Italian cuisine that was served. In many ways, it reminded her of Valentina's, with its checked tablecloths, potted dwarf olive trees and exuberant staff. Yet it couldn't temper her longing for the good old days in Rome with Andre and Uncle Benito and the others.

Before Paris had happened. Before Ben and Avery had been killed.

She reached her house—a small three-bedder in a quiet crescent overlooking Argyle Street, and walked up onto the porch, turning her key in the lock. She didn't bother with the hallway light, just kicked off her shoes by the door, the steam of a hot shower calling her.

Tossing her bag onto the sofa as she passed the lounge-room, she walked into the tiny, dated bathroom with its 1970s mosaic tiles and pink shower bath and turned the light on. Her thoughts had been stirred up by the busy main street and the sounds of all those people, too reminiscent of Paris, and she was restless and jumpy.

It was exactly how she'd felt when she'd arrived home after attending Avery's funeral —wired, unable to settle. She'd attended Ben's funeral too. Then, to her parents' bewilderment, she'd thrown her still-packed suitcase into a rental car, declaring she was leaving again.

'What do you mean you're leaving? You just got home,' her mother had said, looking confused. 'Where are you going?'

'Camden.'

Grace had inhaled sharply. '*Camden*? But that's over an hour away. Who do you know out there?'

'No one. That's the point.' She'd been unable to fully comprehend it herself, only that she'd needed a circuit breaker. Something drastic to circumvent the guilt and loss, the ache, and the memories. Camden was far enough out of Sydney to do that—a semi-rural town nestled on the flood-plains of the Nepean River, with its rolling green hills and historic homesteads. When it wasn't a haven for revellers at night, it was sleepy and recuperative, with gossamer mists over bucolic fields and friendly people. There were hip cafés and antiques stores, and mazes of laneways that scribbled through the town, an equestrian park and a country showground tucked away behind it all. A nice place to hide.

She ran the hot water and stripped off her splattered chef's whites, tossing them onto the floor.

'Therapy would be better than running away,' her mother had said. 'You need to talk to someone.'

Belle stepped into the shower and squeezed her eyes shut.

'I know a good PTSD therapist who the courts work with,' her father had added, so kindly that her heart had hurt. 'It could help with the nightmares.'

She shook their voices away with the hot burn of the water, steam rising quickly, filling the bathroom. Rising like gunfire smoke in a packed café. Ben sitting across from her, sipping his third scotch, and grinning lopsidedly. How she wished she could go back to that night, to know the kind of evil that had been lurking. If only she'd dragged him out of the Papilles sooner, insisted that she leave to meet Andre. If only Ben and Avery hadn't been there at all.

They were in Paris because of me.

She scrubbed her hair, drowning out the memories in the smell of rose shampoo, then lathered it with conditioner. After she was washed and smelling less like tomatoes and garlic, she dried herself, pulled on pyjamas, and climbed into bed. It was one am, and she thought of Kieran and the others, knocking back shots and dancing on the dancefloor, like normal people. She took no comfort in her safe bed, isolated and lonely. She yearned for company, for the presence of another—like Riley, far away in Perth, or Andre, even further away in Rome.

She yawned, burrowing down into her bed, exhaustion

settling at the edges of her consciousness. Sleep prevailed and despite her resistance, she was pulled into it.

BELLE'S EYES FLEW OPEN.

The room was dark and it took her a moment to recall where she was. She glanced around, her heart racing, her head beating a dull tattoo. The bed covers were twisted around her legs, and she gulped back air, the gritty floor of the Papilles Café on her tongue, gunfire residue in her lungs.

You're okay. She swallowed thickly. *You're home. It was just a dream.*

But her fear lingered, and her skin prickled with the breeze on Avenue George V, as though she were still there. The nightmares always took her back—the laughter in the laneways, the music lilting from balconies, the conversation in the alfresco, Ben across from her, nursing a scotch and a bruised ego, asking her to start again with him, just like he'd done on that fateful night. Then the shots would blast, echoing down the avenue and she'd shout at him. *They're coming!* But her voice was always soundless in those dreams, words lost to the past.

She usually woke just before the gunmen opened fire. And all she was left with was the excruciating weight of her guilt, with no chance to say sorry to Ben or Avery, to save them.

Belle untangled her legs from the sheets and reached across for the bedside lamp, flicking it on. A soft glow chased the shadows away and her bedroom filled with reassuring light, a million miles from Paris. She climbed out of bed, her feet touching the cool floorboards, and walked into the kitchen, switching the light on. As she filled a glass with water from the tap and drank it, she stole a glance at the oven clock. Four am.

Outside her window, the streets were quieter. The revellers had gone home, the bars were closed. Camden was peaceful again and she relaxed into it, wondering for the millionth time when the backfire of a car's exhaust or a scream in the crowd wouldn't chill her blood anymore. When she wouldn't be held hostage by her anxiety.

She set the empty glass in the sink and trudged back to her bedroom. There was little chance of returning to sleep; she'd never been able to, not after one of those dreams. She considered calling Andre. It would be eight pm in Rome and he'd be working, or he might have the night off. She longed to hear his voice, to ward off the ghosts, but he would realise the time where she was, would know she was up because of a nightmare, would want to talk about it, would worry himself silly.

No, best to call him when it wasn't the middle of her night. Nothing could come from alarming him. She climbed back into bed, trying to ignore the pang of loneliness in her chest. She would lie there instead, with the light on, until her alarm sounded in three hours, when she'd have to haul herself up to do laundry and grocery shopping, then a shift later at The Olive Grove.

She had just closed her eyes, the lamp glowing softly against her eyelids, when her phone rang. Belle rolled over and snatched it up, wondering if somehow Andre had sensed that she'd needed him. But 'Mum' flashed across her screen instead.

She answered it quickly. 'Hello?'

'Belle.'

'Mum? It's four am. What are you doing up?'

'I'm sorry to call you so early,' her mother said.

'It's all right, I was awake. What's wrong?'

Grace's voice shook. 'It's your father. He's had a heart attack.'

AFTER HANGING UP THE PHONE, Belle dressed swiftly. Her heart was in her throat, her hands shaking as she stuffed clothes and toiletries into a small suitcase, having decided already that she would stay at her parents' house, closer to the hospital. Although the conversation with her mother had been brief, there could be no mistaking the seriousness of it.

'We're at the Royal North Shore Hospital,' she'd quickly relayed. 'They're trying to stabilise him now. I'll call you when I know more.'

Belle tried to marshal her panicked thoughts into order as she stepped outside, the dawn air glacial on her skin. The windscreen was thick with early morning frost when she climbed into the car, and she flicked the wipers on, rubber squeaking against the glass. Spring had arrived the week before, but the mornings were still cold, winter slowly and arduously prising its fingers from the southern world.

She swung the car out of the driveway, down the hill and onto quiet Argyle Street, rolling past Camden's patchwork of laneways and heritage buildings. As she left the main thoroughfare behind, fine mist blanketed green fields, a faint blush in the sky. The hour was still early, with barely another soul on the road, and she would have embraced the tranquillity had her father not just suffered a heart attack.

She navigated onto the motorway as quickly as the speed limit allowed, the sky finally lighting and peak hour stirring to life. An hour later, she reached the Royal North Shore Hospital in St Leonards and parked her car in the underground carpark. She located the intensive care unit, a place she'd hoped never to visit again after Paris and from there, the cardiothoracic ward. Eventually, she found her mother sitting on a chair by her father's bedside, her spine straight, as though poised to react at any moment.

Edward was sleeping, looking uncharacteristically frail beneath a crisp hospital blanket, a plethora of beeping machines connected to him. His face wore the grey, chalky pallor of someone very ill, and she had to swallow down the panic that rose in her throat.

'Mum?' Her voice was a whisper in the doorway.

Grace turned around, eyes swollen and glazed. 'Sweetheart?' She rose from her seat, gave Edward's blanket a gentle pat, then walked out into the corridor. 'What are you doing here?'

'I came as soon as we hung up.' Belle embraced her mother, feeling her slight frame tremble in her arms. 'Is he okay?'

Grace nodded, then indicated with her head that they should talk somewhere else. They walked to a quiet, sterile waiting room where a small TV hung from a corner, the morning breakfast show playing soundlessly with captions. They sat in chairs, Grace smoothing back wrinkled cream pants, her hair uncombed. 'Goodness,' she said. 'What a night.'

'What happened?' Belle asked.

She exhaled shakily. 'Well, I went to bed around ten. I said good night to him in his office and he seemed fine, a little tired perhaps, but otherwise okay. I woke again around midnight, realising he'd yet to come up and thinking that he'd lost track of time while working.'

'Which he does.'

'Yes,' Grace agreed. 'He does. But when I went to check on him in his office, I found him clutching his chest. His skin was grey, and he was sweating. He just looked at me and I knew.' She took a quivering breath, tears leaking from the corners of her eyes. 'I called an ambulance and told them that I thought my husband was having a heart attack, and they came straight away.'

'Oh, Mum.'

'They said we were lucky. I hate to think what would have happened if I'd called them a few minutes later. Or if I'd gone to bed and slept deeply. I would have found him in the morning...' Her shoulders shuddered and she dug around in her pocket, retrieving a tissue and dabbing her eyes.

'And they confirmed it was a heart attack?'

'Yes. Two blocked arteries.'

Two blocked arteries. A fist of comprehension slammed into her. She wasn't used to ailing health toppling her father, the formidable Edward Hamilton, as sturdy as a fort and yet, the past year had taken its toll on him. She hadn't been the only one to lose Ben; her father had felt the loss just as keenly. At times, she saw how it affected him, the heavy way he carried himself, the absentmindedness in a usually sharp mind.

'He'd been feeling unwell this past week,' Grace said. 'Dizzy and not himself, although no arm or chest pain, none that he mentioned, anyway. I told him he was catching a cold.' Fresh tears spilled onto her cheeks. 'A cold! What a fool I am.'

Belle placed her hand on her mother's shoulder. 'It wasn't your fault. You couldn't have known. If anything, your quick thinking saved his life.'

Grace gave her a small, reluctant smile.

'Will they operate?' Belle asked.

'He's scheduled for bypass surgery tomorrow.' She blew her nose into the tissue. 'They've stabilised him for now. He's just tired.' She let out a long, weary sigh and slumped back into the chair. 'It's been a difficult year. And not just because of Ben. He's been worried about you too.'

'He doesn't have to be.'

'But he does.' Grace's voice broke. 'You've both grown so close since Paris. He knows we almost lost you too.'

Belle chewed her bottom lip to keep her emotion in check, playing with a small tear in the worn vinyl seat cover instead. Repairing the fractured relationship with her father had been Paris's silver lining, if there was one. She'd returned home to a man who called her often, told her he loved her and, more importantly, was proud of her. To lose him now was unfathomable, and she willed all her energy, what little she had left, into her father's recovery. Their time couldn't come to an end. Not now.

'Thank you for coming over,' Grace said, glancing at her. 'I wasn't expecting you to, but I'm glad you're here.'

'It's all right. I would have come no matter what.'

'Do you have a shift today?'

'Later, but I called Carlo and Kieran on the way. I'm going to take a few weeks off. I'll stay with you until Dad gets better.'

'Are you sure?' Grace sat up a little. 'Work won't mind?'

'They understand. And I have lots of leave built up.' She wasn't sure she'd be able to concentrate anyway. And when her father was well enough to return home, she wanted to be there with him.

Her mother watched her closely. 'You work far too hard. I worry you're working yourself into the ground sometimes.'

Belle averted her gaze. If she met Grace's eyes, it would all be there for her mother to see—the loneliness, the guilt.

'Have you spoken to Andre lately?' she asked.

Belle shrugged. 'We catch up when we can. It's difficult with the time difference. When I'm asleep, he's awake, and vice versa.'

'Can he come for another visit? That might help.'

'We've been trying to arrange something, but it's hard for him to get away from Valentina's. It's busy and he needs to help his dad. And he already took three months off earlier in the year to come here.'

That magical three months he'd spent with her in Australia had come and gone too quickly, like a ripple in time. She'd taken him to the mountains and the seaside, lazy days spent together, trying to absorb as much of each other as they could before he left again, and they were resigned once more to phone calls and text messages. Then she'd returned to Europe, spending two weeks in Prague with him, before her savings began to protest, along with The Olive Grove.

Over the past year, they'd given long-distance their best shot, but it had been challenging. It was almost excruciating to love someone as she loved Andre and not be able to see or touch him every day. Their relationship had become a cumulative cycle of time zones and schedules and working around the availability of each other just for a decent conversation. Despite their best intentions, she sometimes thought they were hanging on by a thread. Still, he had a key to her house and her heart, an open invitation always.

Grace looked at her intently. 'You look exhausted. Are you sleeping?'

'Enough.'

'Still having nightmares?'

'They come and go,' Belle said, finally meeting her eyes.

Grace sighed with disapproval. 'I wish you would speak to someone. It could help.'

'I'm okay.'

'It's been a year already.'

'Sorry,' annoyance swelled in her chest, 'I didn't know there was a time limit on bouncing back.'

'Don't give me sass,' Grace retorted. 'You're suffering needlessly.'

Belle closed her eyes and opened them again, steadying her voice. 'Mum, I'm fine. You don't have to worry about me.' She gave her a reassuring smile. 'Let's just concentrate on getting Dad better. We can deal with everything else later.'

TWO

With Edward stable and her mother in need of a shower and rest, Belle drove her home. The house was dark when they arrived, but when Grace flicked on the lights, Belle noticed the paramedics' shoe prints and marks from the stretcher wheels on the polished tiles, evidence of the urgency of the night before.

She glanced down the hall towards her father's office. The door was ajar, and she could distinguish the shadowy form of his desk through the doorway, the laptop still open and glowing, a stack of law volumes beside it, once a sturdy tower, now knocked over, likely when the paramedics had worked to stabilise him. She tried to ignore the image of him clutching his chest, skin grey, breathing shallow, then her mother's shock at discovering him, the dread that must have flooded her body.

Belle's stomach churned. It tore at her to see him broken and frail when she'd only ever known him to be a powerhouse.

Her mother touched her arm. 'Can I make you something to eat?'

Belle was brought back to the present. 'No thanks. I'm not really hungry.'

'Neither am I.' Grace smiled ruefully. 'But we can pretend.'

They walked arm in arm to the kitchen. Grace dropped her handbag on the table and went to the coffee machine, turning it on, while Belle contemplated making an omelette.

'He's going to be all right, isn't he?' Her question squeezed her heart as she searched for eggs, chives, ham, and mushrooms in the fridge. She wasn't sure she wanted to know the answer.

But Grace looked optimistic as she returned with two tall mugs of hot coffee and set them on the bench. She slid onto a seat, watching as Belle found a knife and began slicing the mushrooms. 'He's certainly not out of the woods, but he's in good hands. When he leaves hospital, he's going to have to slow down, maybe even retire. He's not a young man anymore. And the last year has been hard...' She trailed off, meeting Belle's eyes. 'For everyone.'

Her words plucked a string deep in Belle's core. The last year had been one long nightmare—the trauma of what had happened in Paris, losing Ben and Avery, starting over again in Sydney, and desperately missing Andre and Riley. No one had escaped unscathed. Riley had become a recluse too, and Andre still grieved for his cousin. Now her father had suffered a heart attack. That night in Paris may have been a year ago, but its effect still rippled across their lives like a pebble skimming a pond.

'I saw a "for sale" sign out the front of the terrace last week,' Grace said. She was referring to Ben's terrace in Pyrmont and her tone was gentle, as though she knew she was traversing sensitive ground.

Belle heated a frypan on the stove and tipped the mushrooms in, then cracked eggs into a bowl, whisked them and set them aside. 'Yes. Penelope and Robert told me they were putting it on the market.' She collected a wooden spoon from the utensils drawer and stirred the mushrooms. 'They asked me again if I wanted it.'

'And you said no?'

Impatience edged her voice. 'I can't go back there.'

'I know,' she said quickly. 'I'm not judging you. I just thought maybe after a year, you'd feel differently. You loved that house and despite the way Ben ended things with you, you still had twenty wonderful years with him. He was your best friend. I don't want you to regret not hanging onto it. Once it's gone, it's gone.'

Ben's parents had been at a loss as to what to do with the Pyrmont terrace after he had died. They'd held onto it for a year, offering it repeatedly to Belle, hoping she'd move back in. They'd told her that it was what Ben would have wanted. And it probably would have been except she couldn't even drive down that street, see the tall weeds in the front garden and the empty spot where Ben used to park his car. How could she move back there after everything that had happened, only to revisit his ghost time and again in every room? To hear his laughter in the walls and his voice in the shadows?

'No, I can't move back there,' she said, removing the mushrooms from the pan and pouring the egg mixture in, swirling it to cover the base. She chose a spatula from the drawer. 'I hate letting them down, but I can't.'

'Do you feel responsible for Ben's death? Is that it?'

The question caught her off guard. 'I just miss him, and I can't go near the house.'

'I don't think that's the whole truth,' Grace insisted. 'You feel responsible for Ben and Avery's deaths. It's why you haven't been able to move past this. But you must realise at some point that none of it was within your control.'

'Can we drop this please?'

'You didn't pull the trigger and you didn't detonate that bomb. You can't control everything.'

'For God's sake, Mum!' The spatula dropped from her hand and clattered on the floor.

Grace sucked in her breath, staring at her daughter.

Belle snatched up the spatula and washed it under the tap. She knew what her mother was doing, coaxing her to confide, but it wasn't going to happen. The last thing she wanted to do was talk about Paris. She never wanted to talk about it again. 'I'm sorry. I shouldn't have snapped.'

Grace sighed. 'No, I'm sorry. I don't mean to push.'

'Yet you do. And everything you say makes sense but I still... I can't...' She put her hands on the bench and let her shoulders sag and her head drop. Exhaustion cradled her muscles and swirled behind her eyes and while she longed for sleep, it would never be so gracious as to grant it to her peacefully.

She heard Grace leave the chair and arrive at her side, her hands on Belle's arms. 'Take a seat. Drink your coffee. I'll finish up here.'

Belle left the stove and walked to the bench, climbing onto a chair, and wrapping her hands around the tall mug as her mother finished the omelette. Grace slid it onto a plate and pushed it across the bench with two forks, perching on the seat next to Belle. 'Want to share?'

Her smile was sad, and Belle knew they were thinking the same thing. As lovely as that omelette looked, neither of them had the appetite for it.

'It's nice to have someone cook in this kitchen again,'

Grace said, sipping her coffee. 'I haven't done much of it lately.'

'Sometimes cooking is the only thing that makes me feel normal,' Belle said.

'I knew early on that you had a gift for it.' Her mother picked up her fork and played with the prongs. 'You took to it like a duck to water. You weren't happy unless you were making something. And Lord knows, I'm not much of a cook. You taught yourself. You were a natural.'

'Did Dad ever cook with me?' Belle asked.

Grace set the fork down, brows drawing together as though the question had surprised her. 'Your father? No, he never cooked in here with you.'

'Oh, I just assumed that's who I inherited my love of cooking from. Dad's side.'

Grace cleared her throat and sipped her coffee.

'Was it Dad's side?' Belle persisted.

Grace averted her gaze. 'It wasn't... I mean, I'm not sure. It was from someone down the line, probably on your father's side. A great aunt possibly.' She gave an uneasy laugh. 'It's hard to keep track.'

'I can't see how it would be,' Belle said. Her mother's sudden aloofness caused unease to slip up her spine. 'Didn't you ever discuss it with Dad when I showed an interest in cooking?'

Grace gave an airy wave. 'I can't remember. It was a long time ago.'

'How can you not remember?' She knew she was pressing, and she couldn't say why exactly, only that she'd inadvertently tapped into something, and an internal alarm had sounded.

Grace tut-tutted. 'Goodness, Belle. Why is this an issue suddenly? You're making a fuss out of nothing.'

'It was just a question.' One that her mother was evading.

'Well for no reason at all, it's become a mountain out of a molehill.' Her tone was curt as she pushed her coffee away and stood. 'I'm going to have a shower, then we can go back to the hospital. Try to eat before we go.'

Her smile was strained as she left the room.

AFTER LUGGING her bag upstairs and into her old bedroom, Belle showered and changed, then went to find her mother. She discovered her in her room, packing an overnight bag for Edward.

Their earlier conversation in the kitchen had left Belle unsettled and she couldn't explain why, only that there was something about it that felt unfinished, the hint of a door opening that now refused to close.

Grace glanced up from folding a pair of pyjamas and placing them into the bag. 'Did you eat some breakfast?'

'I had a little of the omelette.' Belle sat on the edge of the bed and smoothed her hand over the dark grey coverlet. The carpet was grey, so too were the walls. The entire room was like a brooding sky—conservative and Edward.

Grace sighed and ran a hand through her wet hair. 'That shower was good. I almost feel human again.'

'You should stay and sleep. I'll go to the hospital and sit with Dad.'

She shook her head. 'No, I want to go. I'll finish packing his bag, then we can head over.'

Belle watched her add socks and toiletries before clearing her throat. 'Mum, about before, in the kitchen.'

Grace glanced up. The pinched look returned to her face. 'Which part?'

'The part where I asked you who I inherited my love of cooking from, and you didn't seem to like the question.'

Grace blinked rapidly, then returned her focus to the bag. She stared at it for some time before shaking her head with a small laugh. 'Silly me, I packed your father's jeans. He won't need jeans. Well, not yet anyway. Maybe an extra pair of pyjama bottoms would do.' She moved to a chest of drawers and, with her back to Belle, rifled through a pile of Edward's flannel pyjamas. 'Oh look, these are his favourite.' Although her back was still to Belle, she couldn't miss the way her mother's hands shook as she pulled out the pants and pushed the drawer closed.

'Mum.'

Grace's shoulders sagged, her head drooping.

'Mum?' Belle's voice was firmer this time. She loved her mother and the idea of upsetting her wasn't one she took pleasure in, but something was amiss.

Grace turned around with such a grave countenance that it caused Belle's heart to race. She carried herself heavily towards the bed and sat down beside Belle, looking small and defeated, her hands clenched in her lap.

'Mum, talk to me,' Belle pleaded. 'What's going on?'

Grace met her eyes. 'It's not an easy thing to talk about.'

'What isn't easy?' Belle was sitting on the edge of the bed now, spine rigid, imploring her mother to explain.

Grace shook her head as she blinked back tears. 'I did a terrible thing.'

Her voice was so subdued that Belle had to strain to listen. 'What did you do?'

'I'm not that person.' Her voice grew desperate. 'I'm really not. But I slipped.'

'Slipped? I don't understand.'

Grace stood and collected a tissue from the tissue box on her nightstand. She blew her nose, her fingers trembling. When she finally met Belle's eyes, there was a depth of sadness to them that Belle couldn't interpret. 'I suppose there's no point burying it any longer. Lord knows you're old enough to know the truth. You were always old enough and I should have told you. I meant to, but...' She stemmed the tears from her eyes with the tissue. 'But he didn't want you to know.' She returned to the bed and sat down again. Her stare was blank, as though she was lost in the past, no longer in the present.

'Who didn't want me to know? And know what?' Belle asked, frustrated. 'Mum, you're talking in riddles.'

'I know. I'm sorry.' She drew a raspy breath. 'I was aware this day would come, but time hasn't afforded me the right words.'

'Then just say it, however you like.'

Grace nodded. 'Sweetheart, when I was younger, much younger, I had an affair.'

Belle blinked, those four little words sinking into her subconscious. 'An affair?'

'Yes,' Grace said. 'A long time ago. Before you were born. Before I was married, even.'

'An *affair*?' Belle repeated. The word seemed out of place in her father's bedroom, with its proper grey coverlet and moody walls, while she sat next to her pristine mother, her hands still clasped firmly in her lap.

'It was fleeting, and it was a mistake,' Grace admitted. 'I lost control.'

'But if you weren't married, how could it be an affair?'

'I was engaged,' she clarified, 'to your father. So yes, I was unfaithful. I fell in love with someone else.'

'Oh.' Belle tried to process what her mother was saying. She'd cheated on Edward, had fallen in love with another man. 'Did Dad know?'

Grace nodded. 'Yes. I told him everything.'

'And what did he say? Clearly, he forgave you, for you still got married.'

'He forgave, but he never forgot. How can one forget something like that?'

Until recently, finding any common ground with her father had been a challenge, but Belle was overcome with a newfound respect for him. She knew what he must have felt, the betrayal and humiliation of a straying partner, for she'd experienced it when Ben had cheated on her with Olivia. In the same breath, she sympathised with her mother. Edward Hamilton was not an easy man to live with, and she imagined he'd been that way even in his youth.

She reached for her mother's hand and squeezed it. 'It was a long time ago. You were young and people make mistakes. Please don't tell me you've been dragging this around with you all these years.'

A single tear spilled onto Grace's cheek. She dabbed at it with the back of her hand. 'There's a little more to it than that, I'm afraid.'

Belle's heart picked up pace again. 'Okay...'

'Shortly after the affair ended, I discovered I was pregnant.'

Her breath caught somewhere in her lungs, neither able to inhale nor exhale. She knew what her mother was about to say before she even uttered the words. 'Don't.'

Grace stifled a sob. 'I'm so sorry, darling.'

'Don't say it.'

'I should have told you sooner.'

Air rushed through her ears, her pulse quickening. She

gripped the edge of the bed, trying to anchor herself, but the room closed in around her. 'You fell pregnant with *me*?' She had intended to roar the words, but they sounded meek and disbelieving.

Grace nodded. 'Yes.'

'So Dad is not... he's not my...'

Her mother closed her eyes. 'No.'

Belle's mouth hung open. She was certain she was having an out of body experience, watching the scene from afar. It was too bizarre to be real, too confusing. And yet, this was happening. This was her mother telling her that her father was not her father. After all these years! That some other man was. Someone she'd had an affair with. Someone she'd once loved.

All her life Belle had been Edward's daughter. Edward's disappointment. They may have made amends in recent months, but now the penny dropped. She hadn't been his at all. Instead, she'd been everything about that affair. Every day he'd stared into her eyes, reminded of his wife's infidelity, the product of her betrayal. And while he'd still cared for Belle, provided for her, given her his name, he'd also lied to her. They both had.

Belle's thoughts swarmed like a hive of bees. She rose woodenly from the bed and backed towards the door, her hand finding the door frame.

'Belle?' Grace's eyes were pleading. 'Let me explain.'

'There's nothing you could say that would make this better.'

'But I—'

Belle held up her hand. 'Save it.' She turned and left the room.

THREE

Belle strode into her bedroom, snatched up her suitcase and hauled it onto the bed. She unzipped it and began throwing back in the few things she'd taken out of it.

Her mind was a tangle of questions, but she couldn't be in the same room with her mother to ask them. Not just because of the affair—although now that Belle had had time to process it, it was equally disappointing, given what she'd been through with Ben—but because her whole life had been a lie. Every memory, every moment, she had to reassess because the man she'd thought was her father was someone else entirely. She'd been deceived for thirty-seven years.

'Belle.' Grace was at the door, then by her side, her hand on the bag. 'Please don't leave.'

'I'm going home,' Belle said, ripping it away from her. 'I can't be around you.'

'At least let me explain. There's so much you need to know.'

'You lied to me! My whole life—'

'I know.' Grace dipped her head. 'I know. But before

you leave, at least hear me out. Then if you still want to go, I won't stop you.'

Despite her hurt and anger, curiosity nudged at the corners of her brain. The desire to know the truth was a far stronger lure. She let go of the suitcase but her back remained tense. 'Fine.'

Grace gave her a small smile and sank onto the edge of the bed. Belle lowered herself beside her, leaving a good distance between them. Sunshine lit up the walls, chasing the shadows away. The light was an affront, a brilliant blue sky outside that should have been weeping with rain clouds instead, given all that Belle had just learned.

Grace dragged in a tremulous breath. 'I want you to know that none of this was as black and white as you might think it was. It was complicated and confusing, and we all paid the price for that one mistake.'

Belle stared at the floor. She could feel her mother's eyes boring into her, begging her to meet her gaze, but she couldn't. She wasn't ready to forgive, to understand, to sympathise. For now, she just needed the facts.

'I was young, only eighteen when I met your father. Edward, I mean,' Grace said. Her fingers were knotted together in her lap. 'He was a little older than me and a lawyer back then. It was impressive how he'd worked a courtroom—ambitious and competitive. I was captivated by him, and I fell quickly.' She smiled sheepishly. 'I always loved the idea of love. I wore my heart on my sleeve. You're a lot like me in that way.'

Belle could tell her mother was trying to draw comparisons, to bridge the gorge that now divided them, but she wasn't ready to celebrate their similarities. She could never do what Grace had done—lied, cheated.

'After a year, he asked me to marry him.' She wrapped

her arms around herself. 'The bubble didn't last. He worked long days, late nights, always on the weekends. I soon discovered what it meant to be someone's second choice. Your father's career came first, and he made no apologies for that. You can't imagine how lonely that was for me.' She shook her head. 'I'm not making excuses. What I went on to do was wrong, but I was lost.'

Belle felt herself soften infinitesimally. She could imagine how lonely it was because Ben had been the same. Married to his work. Ambitious and focused. Towards the end of their relationship she'd felt it too, the loneliness, unsure of where she'd fit into his life, second to his career. 'Did you ever talk to Dad about it?' Curiosity was getting the better of her and despite the hurt, she felt her anger diminish.

'A few times, yes, but he asked me to be more understanding, that it wouldn't always be that way. That it was stressful studying for the bar while working day and night and I should be patient. Once it was all over, he assured me he'd have more time. Closer to the wedding, though, I was starting to seriously doubt whether that would be the case.'

'So you had an affair with someone else?'

Grace shook her head, wincing. 'No. It wasn't like that. I asked your father to take a trip with me. We needed time away together. But, of course, he said no, he was too busy. I didn't have a lot of girlfriends who were free to go with me at the time, so I went on my own. To Scotland.'

Belle narrowed her gaze. 'You went all the way to Scotland by yourself?'

'I could have visited somewhere closer,' Grace conceded, 'but I'd always loved the idea of Scotland. The castles, the history, the rugged moors. And your father had shown no interest in going there for our honeymoon. He'd wanted to stay close to home so that he wouldn't be too far away in case he was called back to work, so this was my only chance.'

Sympathy niggled at Belle's shock, chipping away at it a little. She was seeing her mother for the first time, not as someone who'd dried her tears and cleaned her grazes, who'd made school lunches and read her bedtime stories, but as a woman, a lover, a person who'd had needs and desires like everyone else. And she'd needed her fiancé to love her, to show her attention.

'I told him I'd get out of his hair for a couple of months, go to Scotland, then I would come back, and we'd marry. Honestly, he looked relieved to have me out of the way.'

That sounded like her father.

Grace made a tsking sound. 'I'm sorry. I'm painting an unfair picture. Your father wasn't as stuffy as that. Maybe if I'd been more independent with a career to match his, I wouldn't have felt so forgotten.'

'Mum, you weren't even married, and already he was making you feel second best. You should have been the most important thing in his world.' She remembered the early years when her relationship with Ben had been at its strongest. He'd showered her with love and affection, despite crawling his way up the corporate ladder. The honeymoon days. Yes, they'd eventually fizzled into heartbreaking infidelity, but she'd had good years with him too, ones she wouldn't have traded for anything.

'Your father loves me, sweetheart. He always has. And he loves you too.' Grace's tone brooked no argument, only conviction. 'When I arrived in Scotland, I worked my way south from Glasgow to a fishing village on the Solway Coast called Kirkcudbright. Spelled not as it sounds—kir-cud-bright—but rather kuh-koo-bree. A delightful little place, although there wasn't much there.' Her eyes glazed over as she reminisced. 'A bed and breakfast, a pub with a restaurant, a school and church, a high street. But it was quaint and colourful and arty. The people were lovely, and I ended up staying for two weeks.'

Her arms were still wrapped around herself, but they seemed to relax a little as she became lost in her memories. 'I met a man there. He worked at the local inn—The Selkirk Arms, if I remember. He was the chef. I ate there often, as did everyone. There weren't many other places to eat at the time. He came out to my table one night and we got talking. We quickly became friends. He was my age, single, quite the dish.' Grace blushed and so did Belle. 'After those two weeks, I told him I was moving on and he asked if he could join me.'

'Just like that?' Belle asked. 'Did he know you were engaged?'

'I wore my engagement ring, yes, and our relationship was entirely platonic at that stage. We'd talked a lot about places in Scotland to visit, and he wanted to play tour guide. Although there was an attraction, I never thought...' Grace bowed her head. 'I never intended to betray your father. That's not what I went there for. But after a couple of weeks on the road together, we became closer and it just happened, one day up north in the Highlands, when the rain came down and we weren't able to go outside.'

Belle looked away until she felt her mother's hand reach across the gap to hers. She glanced back to find tears in Grace's eyes.

'I was so lonely, sweetheart. And this man, this wonderful man I'd met, your biological father, was so good to me. I'd never been one for love at first sight since I'd spent a long time learning to love Edward, but I was swept off my feet so suddenly that I couldn't tell the ground from the sky. Our time together was brief, only a couple of months, but that man was everything to me. It killed me to leave him.' Her eyes were full of anguish. Belle saw the pain and longing in them. 'But, of course, I had to. Edward was waiting for me at home.'

'How did you know I belonged to that man and not Dad?' she asked as she still tried to come to terms with what it all meant. Her dad was not her dad, someone else was—a Scottish man. A chef. It all made sense now, except none of it really did.

'When I got home and I missed a period, I realised straight away I was pregnant. Your father and I hadn't been intimate in months. I knew you weren't his.'

'So you told Dad the truth?'

Grace shrugged. 'Not at first. I was terrified. I thought many things, awful things, about how I could fix the situation. I'd considered sleeping with your father and passing you off as his. But I couldn't live with that lie forever. There had already been too much deceit. So I told him the truth.'

'But you could live with telling *me* a lie? That came easily to both of you.' The anger returned, swelling inside her as she fought to keep the accusation out of her voice. She was broken-hearted but picking another fight with her mother wouldn't give her the answers she needed.

'I know you're hurt,' Grace said. 'This is a lot to take in.'

'It's my whole life, Mum. Everything I've ever known...' She closed her eyes, wondering if somehow she'd fallen into another nightmare, one where Paris didn't haunt her, but her own existence did. The very threads that wove her together weren't as steadfast as she'd once thought. They were a complete and utter fabrication. She'd been nothing more than someone's mistake.

'You must hate me,' Grace said, shamefaced. 'Your father did for a while too. He was livid when I told him, didn't talk to me for weeks—a wall of cold silence.' She shook her head. 'I thought for certain the wedding would be off, but then he came to me a few weeks later and said he loved me and still wanted to get married. I was shocked.'

'And he was happy to raise me as his own?'

'Yes, but on two conditions,' Grace said. 'I was never to contact your real father again and you were never to know the truth. If I agreed to both, he would love and provide for you as if you were his own.'

'And you agreed to that?' The condemnation crept back in.

'I didn't feel I had much of a choice,' Grace said, voice rising. 'I was torn between returning to Scotland to a man I loved, but not knowing if he would want our child, or staying with your father, who I also loved and who loved me. I wanted the best for you and that was what Edward was offering. Stability, a home, a father. So I stayed.'

'Yes, but at what cost?' Belle asked sharply. There had been many times in her life when she'd felt confused by Edward's treatment of her, felt his disappointment undermine her confidence, leaving her afraid to trust her instincts. He'd been hard on her because he'd been desperate to stamp out another man's genes and force the Hamilton into her. Desperate to make her a lawyer and not a chef because his pride had taken a beating with his wife's betrayal. Or perhaps, in the end, no matter how hard he'd tried, he just couldn't love another man's child.

All the headway they'd made in the past year fell away as she contemplated every conversation, every moment they'd shared, pulling it apart like a jigsaw puzzle and trying to fit it back together with the knowledge that she wasn't his.

'I know he hasn't been the easiest person to live with. Believe me, I do,' Grace said, 'but he's struggled with this too. We all have. Although he had the best intentions, maybe it was too much to ask of him.'

'What? To love me like his own? He made me pay every day for *your* mistake.' Frustration surged again even as Belle tried to swallow it back.

'You have to admit, this past year the two of you have been closer than ever.'

'This past year out of how many years?' Belle shot back. 'I never felt good enough for him and now I know why. And you just watched. You never told me the reason.'

Grace hung her head, tears dripping onto her lap. 'I won't lie. You've reminded him every day of my infidelity. I can't take any of it back, I can't fix it. I'm just so sorry.'

Belle tried to quell her bitterness. What was done was done. A fleeting affair thirty-eight years ago had shaped her life, had shaped them all. It couldn't be erased or fixed. A lie had snowballed for the better part of four decades and only time would tell if she could make peace with it. 'Why didn't you have other children? Maybe another child would have made him happier and taken the pressure off me.'

Her mother's eyes grew sad again. 'Your dad couldn't have children. We found out a few years later when we failed to conceive. He had a test and...'

'You should have told me sooner. All of it.' She didn't realise her hands were clenched into fists in her lap until she looked down.

'Yes,' Grace said.

'I shouldn't have to find this all out at thirty-seven years of age.'

'I know.'

'What gave you the right?' she demanded. 'Shame on the both of you.'

Grace choked back a sob.

The sound of a phone ringing down the hall shattered the tension. Her mother stood. 'I better get that.' She hurried out of the bedroom, leaving Belle to stare at her packed bag, wondering where she went from here. Should she stay or relocate to a hotel? Should she go back to Camden? How did she piece her life back together after a single thread had unravelled it?

Her mother's footsteps returned quickly along the carpet. Belle could hear her before she saw her, finally emerging in the doorway, flushed, still gripping the phone. 'It's the hospital,' she said, her voice cracking. 'Your father. We need to get back there now.'

FOUR

Belle and Grace hurried back to the hospital, but as the morning sun embraced the day, Edward never woke to see it. There were no final goodbyes to accompany his last breath as he stepped from this life into the next, just the earth-shattering news that his weak heart had given up, and he'd slipped quietly away.

The coronary care unit filled with Grace's cries, but Belle, still reeling from earlier revelations, was too numb to do more than hold her mother steady. She'd lost two parts of herself that day—her childhood and her father, the man she'd called Dad, anyway. Somewhere out there was *another* man who shared her genetic makeup, her love for cooking, maybe even her eyes and her laugh. A man who may not know she existed.

After she spent some time with her mother by her father's bedside, she stepped soundlessly into the corridor to call Andre. The moment her father passed, and everything before it, came surging back, visceral, and more powerful than before.

When Andre answered, her voice broke. 'My dad died.'

Despite being woken at three in the morning his time, Andre sounded shocked and suddenly awake. 'What? Oh, Belle. What happened?'

'He had a heart attack last night.' A violent wave of emotion rocked her and the tears she'd tried to hold in came pouring out, noisy sobs from way down in her lungs, pushing up her throat.

'*Mio dio*,' Andre muttered. 'That is terrible. I didn't realise he was unwell.'

'He wasn't. I mean, I guess he was. I don't know.' She tried to stem her streaming eyes and nose with the sleeve of her jumper. 'I'm sorry. I should have waited until the morning to call you. I wasn't thinking. You get so little sleep as it is.'

'Don't be ridiculous. You're more precious to me than sleep. Where are you now?'

'At the hospital. Then I'm going to stay with Mum for a while.' She inhaled slowly, shakily, trying to find space in her lungs for air.

'I'll book a flight over.'

'No, don't book it yet,' she said, even though she wanted him to, more than anything. 'Mum and I have a lot to sort out. It would be a wasted trip for you.'

'How can it be a waste?'

'We have to get Dad's estate in order. There's the funeral to plan and we'll have a meeting with his lawyer. And Mum... she's not good.' A vast sorrow welled inside her as she kept one eye on her from the corridor, still sitting by her husband's bedside. The machines had been switched, the tubes removed. And Grace was still, so very still. 'We won't have a lot of time to spend together.'

'I understand. But I want to see you. You've just lost your dad.'

'I know. And I want to see you too.' Her heart ached for so many things that she was utterly depleted. She wanted to tell him to get on a plane, to hold her hand through it all, but she needed to focus on her mother too. 'Can I let you know soon? It's just all happened quickly.'

'Of course. Be with your mother. Call me later when you can, okay?'

'I will. I love you.' Those three words would never convey exactly how she felt about him.

'I love you too, *bella*.'

THE FUNERAL WAS HELD on a cool morning at the Anglican parish around the corner from their house, drawing many of Sydney's elite to the service—judges, lawyers, politicians. It was the third funeral Belle had attended in less than a year, her loved ones slowly being stripped from the world.

She sat in the front pew with her mother—in the same black dress she'd worn for Ben and Avery's funerals—and listened as her father's colleagues delivered eulogies and the organist played a mournful hymn. She found if she concentrated on the organist, fingers plunging into the keys, she wouldn't have to stare at her father's coffin and think about all the questions she'd never had the chance to ask him. *Why didn't you tell me? Why didn't you let me be me?* And perhaps, the more perplexing one of all, why had she been robbed of the chance to know her real father?

Edward had always been a complex man—hard to love, even harder to be loved by. He'd placed unrealistic expectations on her that, genetically, she hadn't had a hope of achieving. She wasn't a Hamilton—an ambitious lawyer with a burning drive to succeed. She was someone else. Someone gentle and kind, who loved being in the kitchen, who wore her heart on her sleeve. And yet, despite his short-comings, he'd also given her more than any reasonable man should be asked to give another's child—a home, stability, an education, and his name.

For the umpteenth time, she was left bewildered by it all, as though her identity had been wiped clean and it was now up to her to go in search of it. But grief and loss and another shock to her system had left her reeling. She longed to place one foot in front of the other and move forward but just like with Paris, she'd become stagnant again.

She jumped slightly at the touch of a hand on hers and realised the service had concluded.

'It's time to go, sweetheart.' Grace's voice was quiet as a curtain closed over the coffin, ready for cremation, and people rose from the pews.

Belle stepped out into the aisle with her mother, mourners following close behind, soft whispers and the occasional whimper clinging to the damp air in the church. Outside, sunshine was bright, spilling onto the steps. Belle was thankful she'd worn her oversized sunglasses, her eyes too heavy and raw to deal with the daylight.

People stopped to pay their respects. Grace was demure in her grief, a stoic smile on her face, a facade to mask the pain. Belle smiled too, mechanically nodding and thanking people, looking forward to the moment when she could slip off her heels, peel off her dress and sink into a hot bath, but knowing they still had the wake to get through.

There was a hand on her back, firm and comforting, and she knew instantly who it was. Riley was beside her, elegant in a black Dior suit. She wrapped her arms around Belle and drew her in for a warm hug.

'You came,' Belle whispered into her shoulder.

'Of course I came,' Riley replied, stroking her hair. She pulled back to assess her. 'How are you holding up, kid?'

Belle shrugged. 'I'm okay. When did you fly in?'

'This morning. I checked into a hotel and came straight here.' Riley shook her head. 'I'm sorry about your dad. It's terrible. The past year has just been terrible!'

Belle gave a small appreciative smile. 'Are you coming to the wake?'

'I'll be there.' She paused, as if scanning the crowd. 'Did Andre fly over?'

'No, I told him to wait,' Belle answered. 'I didn't want to split my focus between settling Mum into life without Dad and having Andre here.'

'I bet he wanted to come anyway.'

'He did. But I didn't want his trip to be filled with sadness.' She glanced back at her mother, still greeting mourners, a long line of them stretching around the church. They were going to be there a while. She sighed heavily, then dug around in her handbag. 'There's still a lot of people to see. Here are the house keys. Do you mind putting the cold platters out? Everything's in the fridge. I'll sort out the hot food when I get there.'

Riley took the keys from her. 'Take your time.'

She trotted down the steps, graceful in her tall heels and smart suit, the sun reflecting off her long, dark hair, and Belle's heart unclenched, glad to have her friend back.

AFTER THE GUESTS had finished eating and they started their first round of coffee, Belle wiped the kitchen bench down, reached for a bottle of wine and a glass and went to sit outside in the backyard. The day had been long, and she'd had little sleep the night before, up until the early hours cooking for the wake. When she'd finally laid her head on the pillow, her thoughts had been too scattered to properly rest.

She found Riley perched on the sandstone retaining wall, an empty glass of wine beside her, her face turned up to the sky. The afternoon light was fading. Gnarled and skeletal trees bordered the yard, stripped bare by winter, waiting patiently for their spring leaves. For some reason, it made her think of Rome and the freezing winter she'd spent there, when snow had fallen and life with Andre had been a sure and magical thing.

All the while believing she knew who her father was.

The thought crept in unbidden, and she quickly shook it away, calling out to Riley. 'Hey.'

Riley blinked and turned to face her. 'Hey, you.'

Belle held out the bottle of wine. 'Top-up?'

'I won't say no.'

Belle filled both their glasses and lowered herself beside Riley. The sandstone was still warm from the day's sun, the winter violas and snapdragons fragrant and colourful. 'Did you eat earlier?'

'I had a few too many of those salmon and avocado tarts. Did you make those?'

'I made everything.'

'They were phenomenal. You must have been cooking for days.' Riley sipped her wine. 'Are you ready for bed yet?'

'I could sleep for a year.' She'd become used to fractured sleep since Paris, but this was on another level. Every muscle in her body felt weighed down by sand, and the sun was too bright for her eyes. She wished she'd thought to bring her sunglasses out. 'How long are you planning to stay?'

'Another week.'

'Then back to Western Australia?' Belle dreaded the answer.

'I guess. Although, if I'm honest, I've found it difficult to settle there.'

'What do you mean?'

'Just that I've tried Perth and Rockingham, then back to Perth, then down to Esperance. All beautiful places, but I...' She shook her head. 'After Paris...'

Belle placed her hand on Riley's. 'I know.'

Vulnerability wasn't Riley's strong suit and she grimaced. 'I still think about that night—searching through the rubble for Andre, losing Avery, not knowing what had happened to you and Ben. Is it just me?'

'No. I think about it too.' Belle shook her head. 'I had no idea you were struggling as well.'

Riley lifted one shoulder. 'Not all the time, but sometimes. I guess we haven't spoken much lately, have we?'

'Not in months.' And she felt Riley's absence like a missing part of her soul—her dry sense of humour, her devastating softness beneath that warrior exterior. Why hadn't she reached out to her sooner? Why had she let all those months slide by? It was just another regret to pile on the others.

Riley gulped back her wine and refilled her glass with the bottle. 'I'm sorry again about your dad. I know you didn't always get along, but he was still your dad.'

Belle looked down into her wine. She hadn't told anyone yet about her mother's affair, that Edward wasn't her biological father. A week later and she was still grappling with it, stepping through all the moments in her life when the truth had been staring her in the face and she hadn't seen it. She'd barely spoken to her mother since she'd been told, not that Grace had been overly talkative the past week, and certainly not about that. When conversation was inevitable, it was restricted to funeral arrangements or what food to serve at the wake or if the other wanted a cup of tea.

Nevertheless, the burden weighed heavily now, the truth like a stone she dragged around with her. Edward was gone and she should have been focusing on closure, but all she could feel was the great gaping hole he'd left behind.

'Before Dad died, my mother told me something,' she said, playing with the stem of her glass, feeling the need to unburden herself now, so one other person could know and feel equally shocked.

Riley glanced her way.

'She confessed that she'd had an affair with another man while engaged to my father.'

Riley's brows shot up, then she broke into a disbelieving grin. 'Wow. Grace.'

'Yeah, not at all like her.'

'How long did it last?'

'About a month or two. She was travelling through Scotland on her own and met a guy, some chef in a restaurant. She was lonely with my dad in those early days. Even before they were married, he could be difficult.'

Riley lifted a shoulder as though it were no surprise to her. 'Why did she marry him if she wasn't happy?'

'Because she fell pregnant to her lover.'

It took a second for the penny to drop, then Riley's eyes bulged. 'Pregnant? You mean...'

Belle nodded. 'I'm the product of that affair. Edward wasn't my biological father.'

Riley looked gobsmacked. 'Wait. How long have you known about this?'

'I found out the day Dad died.'

'A week ago?' Riley's expression darkened. 'You were told a week ago that your dad wasn't your dad?'

'Yes.' She watched the horror on Riley's face, then when the shock subsided, she continued. 'When Mum returned to Sydney, she realised she was pregnant, and she told Dad. He said he would still marry her on two conditions—that she ended all contact with my real father and that I was to never know the truth.'

Riley reached for the wine bottle again and cast a pointed look at Belle's still full glass. 'Drink,' she ordered.

Belle gulped back a mouthful, then thrust the glass forward so Riley could top it up.

Riley then returned the lid to the bottle and set it down on the garden wall between them. 'I don't know what to say. How could they have kept this secret from you? You're not five years old, you're a grown woman. You should have known about this from the start.'

'I've been struggling with it. The relationship I had with my dad wasn't always great, but lately it had been. And all my life we've been so different so the whole thing should make sense now, except it doesn't. And now I don't know whether to feel relieved or confused or sad or angry. I'm just... I'm all over the place.'

'Of course you are!'

'And Mum doesn't want to talk about it. She dropped the bomb and now she's clammed up. All I can think about is this guy,' Belle admitted. 'He's always in the back of my mind. What's his name? What does he look like? Where is he now?'

'You need to ask her about him.'

Belle cringed. 'I know, but I don't want to add to her stress.'

'You need answers.'

'She hasn't brought it up again. I don't think she wants to talk about it.'

'Okay, put it like this,' Riley said, swivelling on the wall to face her. 'Can you go back to your life knowing what you know now and just put it all behind you? Forget you ever knew about this guy? Or will you forever ask yourself those questions?'

She didn't hesitate. 'I'll forever ask myself those questions.'

'Then you need to talk to your mum. Make her give you the answers. Your parents took a critical choice away from you and concealed it your whole life. The least she can do is give you some information.'

Belle took another gulp of wine and nodded. 'Yes, you're right. I'll speak to her.'

'Then afterwards there's just one thing left to consider.'

'Which is?'

'What you'll do with that information.'

FIVE

It took several knocks on Grace's bedroom door the next morning before she opened it. 'Is this a bad time?' Belle asked. She had a cup of tea in her hand for her mother and a stomach full of knots.

'Not at all.' Grace beckoned for her to come inside. She was perched on the edge of the bed, one of Edward's shirts in her lap, her fingers fondly touching the collar, looking as though she'd been lost in a memory. 'Were you standing there for long?'

'Just a couple of knocks,' Belle said. She held out the cup. 'I made you tea.'

Grace placed the shirt down and reached for it. 'Thank you.' She blew on the steam and took a cautious sip. 'I'm sorry. I've been up here a while.'

'It's okay. You missed breakfast. I can make you something if you like.' Her mother had taken to disappearing into rooms and failing to emerge for hours. Like in the office the day before. She'd found her mother sitting at her father's desk, just staring at the laptop, fingers splayed across his law journals.

Grace shook her head, setting the cup on the night-stand. 'I'm not hungry. But the tea is lovely.'

Belle glanced around the room. There was an empty cardboard box beside the wardrobe. 'What are you doing?'

Grace's expression was vacant as if she wasn't sure herself. 'I was going to pack away some of your father's things. But then I got here with the box and realised that I'm not sure I can.'

Belle looked inside the wardrobe, a large walk-in where her father's suits and shirts hung crisply, shoes lined precisely along shoe racks, his ties, belts, and scarves neatly draped as though at any moment he would dress for work.

The last book he'd been reading sat on the nightstand, an autobiography, the page still bookmarked, and his slippers were placed next to the bed where he'd left them before he'd suffered his heart attack.

'I didn't think it would be easy, packing his things away,' Grace said, more to herself than to Belle. 'I just thought, little by little, I could somehow do it.'

'You don't have to do anything you're not ready for.' She took the cardboard box and pushed it deep into the wardrobe, to be used another day. 'In fact, this might all be too soon. There's no hurry.'

Grace looked relieved that the decision had been taken out of her hands. 'Yes, you're right. No hurry. I just feel lost without him. And I thought, maybe if I didn't see his clothes every day, I wouldn't feel the ache in my chest.' Her voice wobbled.

'Of course.' Belle returned to the bed and sat beside her. 'I understand.'

'He wasn't the easiest man to live with,' she said, 'and our marriage wasn't without its problems, but I did love him. I feel his absence greatly now.'

'Did you love my real father too?'

Although Belle's tone was kind, Grace glanced at her abruptly, before her countenance softened. 'That was a different kind of love. But yes, what we shared, despite the little time we spent together, was special. I'll always remember it with fondness.'

'I know Dad asked you not to, but did you ever tell that guy about me?'

Grace dropped her gaze to her lap, her hair falling around her face. 'No, sweetheart. I didn't want to deceive Edward any more than I already had. I kept my promise.'

'But you took away a man's right to know his child,' Belle said. Although she hadn't intended it, her voice grew heavy with accusation.

Grace bristled with defensiveness. 'I did what I thought was right at the time, the only thing I could have done.'

'You had choices, Mum.'

'That's easy for you to say. We're all wise after the fact, are we not?'

'All I'm saying—'

'I know what you're saying, Belle,' Grace retorted. 'But what you fail to understand is that I was engaged to one man and carrying the child of another. And although I only had myself to blame, I was terrified. Edward offered me a future and stability, not just for me, but for you. You were the only one I was concerned about at the time. I made those choices for *you*.'

'But you took away my choices at the same time.'

Grace's mouth pulled into a thin line. 'I don't know what you want from me. Sorry won't help, I know that, and I can't take any of it back.'

'I want to find him,' Belle said softly.

Grace flinched as if she'd been slapped. 'What?'

'I want to find my real dad.'

She made a sound like a wounded animal. 'For goodness' sake, Belle.'

'I think after all this time I have a right to know who he is.'

'I understand that, but we haven't even scattered your father's ashes yet. Edward, the man who loved and raised you, hasn't even been gone two weeks.'

'I'm sorry if this hurts you—'

Grace stood suddenly. 'I can't talk about it now.'

'Well, when can you talk about it?' Belle jumped to her feet too.

'When it's not such an insult to your father's memory.'

Belle pressed her lips together, lest another retort came tumbling out. 'Mum,' she said carefully, 'I'm not trying to upset you, but I need to know where I come from.'

Grace frowned. 'You come from me. And Edward raised you. After all these years, isn't that enough?'

Belle desperately wanted it to be, but her life had been tipped on its head. Despite every moment she'd ever spent with her mother and the conversations they'd had, this one thing, this one vital fact had never come up. Ever. How could that be? Just when she thought she could be content not knowing, she was spurred on again by the deceit of it all. 'Right now, no, it's not enough.'

Grace placed her hands on her hips and drew a deep breath. 'Then I need time. Because this is too much too soon. Your father has just died, Belle. Have some respect.'

Guilt forced Belle to bite back her words, even though her mind raced with confusion, hurt and a burning anger. Her mother collected her cup of tea and strode out of the room without a backward glance.

TWO DAYS on from trying to wrangle even a sliver of information from her mother, Belle sat across from Riley at a café table, sipping coffee and tearing strips off a croissant that she had no desire to eat.

'She won't talk,' Belle complained. 'She says she needs more time.'

'She's already had thirty-seven years to tell you.'

'She's grieving. Her life has been turned upside down.'

Riley nodded thoughtfully. 'Well, to be fair, we know how that feels. What are you going to do about it?'

'I want to find him.'

Riley's eyebrows shot up. 'Okay.'

Belle shrugged miserably. 'I mean, I *think* I do. Oh, I don't know.' She was so exhausted it was hard to concentrate. Sleep had become elusive again, as she churned every conversation she'd ever had with her parents over in her mind until it ached. At least it kept the nightmares at bay, for she hardly slept, but it was replaced instead by the shame of never suspecting their lie, never taking a close enough look at her father's smile, the way he laughed or the way he carried himself, to realise how different they were. Why hadn't she noticed before?

'At the end of the day,' Riley said, 'you have to do what feels right for you. You're the one who has the most to gain or lose here. If you want to wait until the timing feels better, do that. If you want to find your father now, you should start. Who knows how long the process could take?'

The problem was, Belle wasn't sure what she wanted to do. Yes, she had a burning desire to find him, to know him, but the lines were blurred as if she were straddling reality and make-believe. She was desperate to seek out the part of her that she now realised had always been missing, but she was struck by an unshakable obligation to her parents and respecting the life they'd given her.

Belle sighed, picking up her coffee and sipping it. 'I'll wait for Dad's ashes to be scattered, then I'll start. I'm due back at work in two weeks so if I'm going to do anything about it, I need to do it now. I don't think I could wait any longer beyond that. It would just eat at me.'

'Where are you going to start looking for him?'

'Scotland.'

Riley spluttered into her coffee. '*Scotland?*'

'That's where she met him, in a small fishing village.'

'I thought you were going to look for him on the internet.'

'I'll do that too,' Belle said. 'But I want to go to Scotland, to Kirkcudbright first. I'll go wherever I need to go. I'll turn the place upside down if I have to.'

'Then I'm coming with you.'

Overwhelming emotion ached in Belle's chest. She'd missed Riley's fierce loyalty, her protective shadow. 'Are you able to do that? Just go to Scotland with me? What about Perth, your apartment there, your job?'

She shrugged nonchalantly. 'It'll be there when I get back. I have my passport with me. I just have to buy a bigger suitcase and some warmer clothes.'

For the first time in weeks, Belle smiled broadly. 'Okay.'

'But you're going to need his name,' Riley added.

'I know.'

'Do you think your mum will give it to you?'

Belle frowned and picked at her croissant again. 'Probably not.'

SIX

After coffee with Riley, Belle drove back to her mother's house. Up in her bedroom, she glanced at the clock and calculated the time difference with Rome. It was one in the morning there and Andre would be at the staff dinner. She took a gamble, dialling his number, hoping he'd hear his phone above the noise.

He answered on the third ring. '*Ciao*, Belle.' His words were warm, clearly relieved to hear from her.

'*Ciao*,' she replied. Voices and music were loud in the background, and she could hear him shuffling, his chair scraping.

'Just a minute. I will go into the kitchen where I can hear you.'

The noise died away as she heard the kitchen doors squeak open. 'That's better,' he said. 'How are you?'

'I'm good. Glad to hear your voice.'

'Me too. How is your mother?'

Belle sat on the edge of her bed. 'She really misses Dad.'

'When my mother died, I was only young, but I

remember how it almost broke my father. There is grief, then there is adjustment. It all takes time.'

There was also an illegitimate child, but Belle hadn't found the opportunity to tell him yet, so for now, she pushed the thought away. 'How's everything on your side?'

'Good. Valentina's is busy, although we are heading into the cold season now. Hopefully, we will get the ski tourists passing through. And we finally have a dessert menu. You should see it! I'll take a photo and send it to you.'

'I miss you.' The words came gushing out and along with it, a sob that she couldn't contain.

'Oh, *bella*,' Andre said. 'I miss you too, more than anything. More than I can stand sometimes.'

'I just really needed to hear your voice.' Especially after days of pent-up sadness and confusion.

'And I needed to hear yours. But please don't cry. You're breaking my heart.'

She could hear his helplessness, wished he were standing right beside her to wrap his arms around her. What she wouldn't give to bury her head in his chest, to smell the mix of coffee and cologne on his shirt, to have his hands stroke her hair while he told her everything would be okay.

She wiped her eyes, trying to regain her composure. 'I'm sorry. I don't mean to cry in your ear.'

'Don't ever apologise. You're grieving. And that's what I'm here for.'

'There's just been a lot going on. Sometimes I wonder if I can take it anymore.'

'I should come,' he said immediately. 'I know you said it would be a wasted trip, but I want to be there with you. I can get on a flight after the weekend shifts are over.'

She shook her head. 'No, don't do that. Valentina's is busy.'

'I don't care.'

'Well, I do. It's too long a journey for such a short trip. And I might be heading your way soon.'

There was silence as her words settled. 'Heading my way?'

'I'm planning a trip to Scotland.'

She heard him cough in surprise. 'Scotland? Okay.'

'I learned something recently. Something that's changed my life. I'm not who I thought I was.'

'Can you be a little more specific?'

She filled him in on everything she'd discovered recently. 'My father offered to marry my mother and raise me as his own on two conditions.'

'Which were?'

'That she cut off all communication with my real father and that I was to never learn the truth of my parentage.'

There was a low whistle on the other end of the line. 'Oh, Belle.'

'Edward wasn't my biological dad,' she said. 'But do you know what hurts the most? Not the fact that she'd had an affair or that she fell pregnant to someone else, but that they kept it from me. Over three decades later, I stumbled across it by chance.' She let out a frustrated breath.

'Maybe your mother made the only choice she could,' Andre said. 'She was obviously scared. We have to sympathise with that.'

'I do sympathise with that. But they kept it a secret for too long. That's the part I can't reconcile with.'

'Maybe your father wanted to give you the best kind of life without this hanging over all your heads.'

'That wasn't his choice to make,' she argued.

Andre's tone was gentle. 'Belle, people make questionable decisions when they're afraid. I'm not condoning what they did, but it sounds like they did it out of love for you.'

'They took something away from me that wasn't theirs to take.'

'I agree, but what can come from all this anger? It will only hurt you more.'

'I'm going to Scotland,' she said resolutely. 'I'm going to find my real father.'

There was clanging in the background and Uncle Benito said something about the pizza trays. She heard Andre move into the back alleyway behind the kitchen where it was quieter. 'What does your mum think about that?'

'Her whole world's turned upside down. She's not ready for it. But if I'm going to do this, I need to do it now. There's a man out there who's my father and he has no idea I exist.'

'This could upset a lot of people and cause a lot of pain, including for him.'

Belle fell silent, her heart lurching at his words. Andre was right. She wasn't the only one hurting. Her mother was too, and her real father would be devastated once he learned of the news. Or maybe he wouldn't. Maybe he wouldn't want to know her at all, something that she was also forced to consider.

It was hard to know what to do anymore, what would yield the best outcome and cause the least pain. One thing she knew for certain was that she couldn't return to her life in Camden just yet knowing everything she knew.

There was a flurry of noise in the background again, then Andre groaned. 'I'm sorry, I have to go. We need to clean up the kitchen and close for the night. Can I call you later in the week?'

'You can meet me in Scotland instead.'

She felt his grin from across the oceans, dimples deepening, dark eyes crinkling, and she knew his answer before he spoke it. 'Of course I will meet you.'

THE FOLLOWING MORNING, Belle found her mother in the back garden, planting seedlings of beets, cucumber, and tomatoes in the soil. Grace may have been a terrible cook, but she was a proficient gardener, and her garden, whether it be flowers, shrubs, or vegetables, always thrived, no matter the season.

'Sleep well?' she asked, as Belle came down the back steps and onto the flagstone path.

It was still early, the sun pale in a whitewashed sky, a faint sprinkling of frost crystalising the grass. Belle crossed her arms against the chill. 'It was okay.'

Grace patted the earth around a planted tomato seedling. 'Another nightmare?'

She shook her head, then walked closer, pausing by the garden wall where her mother was kneeling. 'Actually, I've been thinking a lot about my dad.'

Grace dusted the soil off her hands and settled back on her haunches, glancing up. 'I understand. I think about him too.'

'I mean my other dad. My real one.' She immediately winced as she said it.

Grace let out a sigh. 'Not this again, Belle.'

'But he's all I can think about. I want to go to Scotland.'

Grace stood abruptly, abandoning the seedlings still left

to be planted, and headed for the back steps as though she could escape the conversation.

'I'll wait for Dad's ashes to be scattered, then I'll go,' Belle said, following her.

Her mother spun around. 'I understand your need to find your real father, but you have to realise he has no idea you exist. He likely has a family of his own now, children, grandchildren even. Do you think turning up out of the blue is a good idea for either of you?'

'You took that choice away from him,' Belle said. 'From both of us. So yes, I do think it's a good idea.'

'And what if he's not in Scotland anymore?' Grace challenged. 'What if he moved, or worse, died?'

'Or maybe he's still where you left him, in that tiny village, happy to finally meet me,' Belle said. Her voice rose and she had to steady it, remembering that it was still early morning and the neighbours might be sleeping.

'I highly doubt it,' Grace mumbled.

'What's his name? At least tell me that so I can look him up.'

Grace bit her lip. 'I told you I need more time before we go down this road.'

'I don't have time,' Belle said shrilly. 'You took decades away from us. And now you're stonewalling me.'

'I'm not doing that,' Grace said. 'I'm just asking for your patience and some respect for your late father. This is a lot for me to deal with as well.'

Belle scoffed. 'What's this really about? Is it about a man you once loved finding out that you kept a daughter from him? Are you ashamed of what he might think of you?'

Grace averted her eyes.

'So this *is* about you?' Belle said.

'It's about everything.' Grace turned back, her eyes

brimming with tears. 'I'm still reeling, Belle. I have barely enough strength to get up in the morning. I know what I did was wrong, and I need to fix that for you, but at the moment, I can hardly breathe. I need time.'

Belle reached for her mother's hand. 'I'm not asking you for anything except his name.'

But the hesitation on her mother's face told her that she wasn't ready to give it.

Belle shook her head with disappointment. 'Don't worry. I'll find him myself.'

SEVEN

They scattered Edward's ashes across the Lane Cove River behind the family home, a place he'd often retreated to, particularly during and after intense court cases. He'd taken Belle with him when she'd been a child, when she'd begged long and hard enough and he'd relented with a grumble. They'd go hiking along the trails of scribbly gums and wattle trees and sometimes, they'd kayak down the river. There were always few words spoken—he'd never been one for idle conversation—but she hoped those times spent together had meant as much to him as they'd meant to her. It was hard to know with Edward.

Grace tipped the container onto its side and carefully tapped the ashes into the water, the gentle tide carrying him out into the middle of the river. The day was glaringly bright, and Belle shielded her eyes with her hand, trying to remember the good times spent with him amidst the more challenging ones. If she found solace in that, maybe she wouldn't need to embark on a journey to find her real father. Maybe she wouldn't have to put Grace through the ordeal or insult Edward's memory. Yet as hard as she tried, all she found was the same yearning curiosity to know the man who had fathered her, irrespective of anything else.

Grace replaced the lid on the container and sighed. She seemed to have aged a hundred years in the past few weeks, eyes sad and wrinkles creeping quietly onto her skin. Belle swallowed back her guilt. Her actions had never been intended to upset anyone, to be interpreted as a lack of love or respect for Edward. Standing there watching her mother's grief and her father's ashes drift downstream, she wondered if she should abandon the idea altogether, until she realised all over again that simply forgetting about it would be like asking the sun not to rise.

Back at the house, Grace filled the kettle with water and switched it on. 'Tea?' she asked.

'I'm going,' Belle said softly.

Grace's eyebrows drew together with confusion. 'Going? You mean home?'

'To Scotland.'

Her mother leaned against the benchtop and stared at her.

'I want you to come with me,' she said.

Grace smiled sadly. 'I've just scattered your father's ashes in the river. To go now and find the man I was unfaithful with...' She shook her head. 'What kind of person would that make me?'

Belle walked to her mother and hugged her tight. 'You're not doing it for you. You're doing it for me.'

'Maybe in a few months we can go.'

Belle pulled away, frustration gnawing at her again. 'I don't have a few months. Right now, it's all I can think about. I can't eat or sleep or concentrate. You dangled this carrot and now you won't support me.'

'I'm sorry about that.'

'Sorry's not enough. Not for what you and Dad took away from me.'

Grace sighed. 'Must we keep having this conversation, Belle? I'm tired. I could sleep for days.'

'Then go to sleep, but I'm still going to Scotland. And I'll do it with or without your blessing. The least you can do is give me his name.'

Her mother seemed to shrink in the room as though all the fight had left her. 'I won't go with you,' she said finally. 'But I'll tell you who he is.'

Belle sucked in her breath.

'The man you're looking for is Callum MacKenzie. He's your biological father.'

His name. Belle's heart stopped. She finally had his name.

LATER THAT NIGHT, Belle booked a flight to Scotland for Riley and herself that departed in two days' time. She also called Carlo at The Olive Grove to ask for two more weeks' leave which he gave her. Then she began searching for her father.

She was cross-legged on her old bed in her parents' house, with the laptop in front of her, deciding she would try her luck with a simple Google search. Her biological father's name was a common one, and when she typed it in, it produced an abundance of results—Callum MacKenzies from all over the world, with varying ages and careers—but the results were too plentiful and there was nothing she could immediately latch on to. After a while, she gave up on Google and tried an ancestry site instead.

She hoped that he or a member of his extended family

would already have a DNA profile available and if she completed a test too, she could be matched to them. If that occurred, maybe a communication channel would open between them and she could track him down. Her already befuddled mind whirred with the possibility of it. But as she explored the site and read all the information, she realised the DNA process could take weeks from start to finish. She would need to wait for the kit to arrive, and there was every chance she'd already be in Scotland before it landed on her doorstep.

She drummed the keyboard with her fingers, thinking. A test like that could certainly yield results, but it could also lead her down false paths. There was no guarantee she would find her father that way. Depending on the DNA matches, she might spend months trying to reach people and they could be so distant in her family tree they may not know her father at all. Once again, *time* came to mind, and she decided that heading directly to Kirkcudbright, where her mother had first met him, was still her best chance. She parked the ancestry site for the time being, intent on coming back to it if Scotland failed, and switched her focus to social media instead.

It turned out there were many Callum MacKenzies on Facebook, and there was no precise way to determine which of them lived in Scotland unless they chose to display their country in their profile. Those who did live in Scotland were plentiful, and it would be a lengthy task to contact them all and establish who had travelled with a woman called Grace over three decades ago. Yet another frustrating dead end.

There was also the possibility that Belle's real father wasn't on social media, which got her thinking about what her mother had said out in the garden. That he may no longer be in Scotland, that he could have died, or he may not welcome the arrival of a long-lost daughter. None of which boded well for Belle's search.

Hours later and with nothing to show for her efforts but strained eyes and a renewed sense of helplessness, she shut her laptop down, hardly able to sleep as images of ancestry sites and her father's name skated beneath her eyelids.

TWO DAYS LATER, she passed much of the flight to Glasgow in the same fashion, unable to relax and trawling through Facebook profiles on the plane's Wi-Fi.

Riley tugged off her eye mask and glanced at her. 'You might want to get some sleep,' she mumbled. 'We're landing in four hours.'

Belle couldn't have slept if she tried. While her brain was desperate to find anything about her biological father, it was also starting to merge and confuse profiles so that all the Callums had begun to look the same. 'I've been thinking, when we land in Glasgow, we should hire a car and head straight to Kirkcudbright. I don't want to waste too much time doing other stuff. I just want to get there.'

'Then what? Ask every person in the village if they know your Callum?'

'Yes.'

Riley tugged the thin airline blanket up to her chin. 'What if he has a wife and children? This will be huge for them.'

'I know,' she said. She thought again of the ancestry site and the DNA test, if she should have taken that safer, slower approach to finding him. Turning up on someone's doorstep and declaring you were their daughter was a bold move. If she stopped to consider the ramifications of that, of what it would truly mean for everyone involved, she would lose her nerve. And maybe she should have thought of the consequences first, but she'd had tunnel vision when she'd learned the truth and had become immediately fixated on finding him. She'd come this far now—four hours out from Glasgow—and she would see it through, even if the whisper of warning in her brain was growing louder by the day.

The remainder of the flight passed ordinarily, with Belle finally falling into a turbulent sleep filled with dreams of Kirkcudbright, pictured exactly the way she'd seen it the thousands of times she'd googled it. She dreamt of a man who walked ahead of her, his profile tall and lean, hair the colour of espresso, like hers, but she could only see the back of him. She called out his name, but he wouldn't slow, wouldn't turn around, wouldn't show her his face, and no matter how quickly she jogged to catch him, he always appeared just out of her reach.

THE PLANE LANDED and they disembarked, moving through customs and quarantine, fetching their luggage from baggage claim. They located the rental car desk, signed the paperwork, and paid the fee.

On the way to collecting the vehicle, Belle called Andre to let him know they'd arrived safely, but it was answered by his voicemail. It was the lunch shift at Valentina's. She knew he'd be behind the bar juggling the espresso machine and several trays of *aperitive* and limoncello, unable to hear his phone. Her heart squeezed at the thought of him, and she pushed down the familiar stab of longing.

The air was bitingly cold when they stepped outside the

airport, Riley rubbing her hands together. When Belle had dashed home to Camden for a bigger suitcase and her passport, she'd remembered that it was autumn in the Northern Hemisphere and had packed warmer clothes. Riley, not having anticipated anything but Sydney spring weather when she'd left Perth, had had to rush to the mall to buy the last of the winter range.

They located the rental vehicle and climbed in, Riley turning the heat up as Belle steered them out of the airport carpark. The sky was grey, the heavy-bottomed clouds thick and foreboding. Riley located the village of Kirkcudbright on her phone and directed Belle away from the city and south towards the Scottish coast.

Belle was grateful to reach the open roads, away from Glasgow's busy streets, as Scotland sprawled around them, an endless slideshow of rolling hills and dense forests. There was the occasional glittering inlet and, at times, the sun peeked through the clouds, casting reluctant slivers of yellow, lighting up the landscape.

It took all Belle's energy to concentrate on driving, as she alternated between excitement at witnessing Scotland's southern beauty and the inevitable approach to Kirkcudbright. She wasn't sure what awaited her there. Would Callum still be working in the same restaurant where her mother had met him all those years ago? The Selkirk Arms? Or would he be long gone? A thousand tiny butterflies beat their wings against her stomach, and she was aware that she'd fallen silent.

'Should we stop for a break?' Riley asked, casting her a dubious look.

'We're thirty minutes out. Let's just get there,' she said with more conviction than she felt. It had all seemed so simple back in Sydney, the only goal being to find him. But so far from home and amidst everything foreign, she was less certain of her decision.

Kirkcudbright was a seaside town on the Solway Coast. They followed the motorway, passing Castle Douglas, all the way to the town's cheerful blend of Victorian, Georgian, and medieval buildings. The River Dee accompanied them on the last leg of the journey, cutting through the village, the walled banks of Kirkcudbright Bay lined with coloured fishing vessels and a rippled current flowing out to the Solway Firth.

Belle's heart quickened in her chest as Riley directed her to the accommodation they'd booked before leaving Sydney. Situated in the heart of the high street, Fable House was a white double-storey Victorian terrace with mint green windowsills bordering pretty sash windows, and a front door of the same mint colour. Tenacious ivy crept up the stone facade all the way to the weathered slate roof, where a row of chimney pots marched along the roofline. Steps, wet with rain, led to the front door and were lined with pots of yellow and white daffodils.

Belle found a parking spot a few terraces down and they rolled their luggage to the bed and breakfast, tugging it up the steps to the door. It was open and they stepped into a small foyer of beige carpet and crisp white walls. There was a faint smell of rosehip and creeping damp, mingled with sea salt from the nearby harbour, but everything appeared neat and clean.

Shuffling down the staircase caught their attention, and Belle and Riley turned. A plump woman in her early seventies with a nest of white hair pulled back into a bun stepped into the foyer. 'Hello there,' she said, with a kind face and pleasant Scottish lilt. 'What kin I dae fur ye today?' She stepped behind the reception desk with a wide smile.

'We have a booking for two nights under Belle Hamilton,' Belle said.

'Let me take a look.' The woman tapped her keyboard, eyes scanning a screen. 'Aye, I see ye here. Two nights. I've booked ye into one of our river view rooms.'

'If we decided we wanted to stay longer, say one or two weeks, would it be a problem?' Belle asked. She'd prepared herself for the worst but was hopeful for the best.

'Ye kin stay as long as ye like, dears. Most of the tourists have gone home. Ye have the place to yerselves.' The woman beamed brightly. She had an affable disposition, her cheeks rosy like red apples and her ample bosom straining against her white blouse. 'Now, I kin see you've already paid fur the two nights, so I'll take ye up to yer room. Did ye come straight from Glasgow airport or have ye been in Scotland a while?' She didn't wait for their answer. 'Ye must be exhausted. Let's go and get ye settled.'

She collected a key from a board of keys behind her and waddled out from behind the counter. 'My name is Mrs Murray, by the way. Ye kin leave yer luggage here and Mr Murray will be along shortly to bring it up to yer room.' She indicated that they should follow her up the staircase but before stepping up, she pointed through a doorway, where the air hung rich and fragrant. 'Through there is the dining room where we serve yer meals if you're eating in. Breakfast is from six. Tea is at seven.'

They followed Mrs Murray up the staircase to the second floor, and she led them down a narrow hallway to one of the doors. 'Here is yer room. I hope ye like it.' She threw the door open to a room of beige carpeting and two-tone painted walls in plum and cream. There was a fireplace on one side and windows overlooking a cluster of slate roofs and the river on the other. Two double beds were draped with matching white eiderdown quilts and a single armchair sat beside a table layered neatly with packets of tea, coffee, and biscuits.

'The bathroom is just down the hall and I'll set out fresh towels fur ye daily,' Mrs Murray said.

'Thank you.' Belle glanced out the window. 'It's lovely.'

'It really is,' Riley agreed.

Mrs Murray grinned so widely that her cheeks shone. 'That's right kind of ye.' She left the key on the table beside the packets of tea and coffee. 'We'll be back up shortly with yer luggage.' She stepped out of the room and closed the door behind her.

Riley flopped down on the bed and yawned while Belle kept her gaze on the village beyond the window. It was small, but the high street was vibrant and cluttered with terraces, art galleries and shops. Across the river, open green fields and houses sprawled under a mellow sky.

A sliver of anticipation ran through her. Was Callum still here? Which house might he live in? Would it be as easy as walking into the Selkirk Arms and finding him there?

Part of her hoped it would be. The other part was just terrified.

EIGHT

'I've put some fresh towels in the bathroom fur ye. And I thought ye might be hungry, so I made ye something to eat too.' Mrs Murray returned shortly after, bustling back through their bedroom door, balancing a tray of sandwiches cut into neat little triangles and a small jug of juice. 'I hope ye like roast beef and chutney.'

She placed the tray on the table. Famished, Belle reached for a sandwich, devouring it in a few quick bites. The beef was tender and the chutney sweet, and Riley must have noticed the look on her face, for she reached for a sandwich too.

Mrs Murray chuckled with delight. 'I'm glad ye like them.'

Behind her, a tall, spry man appeared with their luggage, tugging it through the doorway and leaning it up by the wall. 'This is Mr Murray, my husband,' she said.

'Hullo.' He tipped his cap. 'Welcome to Kirkcudbright and Fable House.' He had kind eyes like his wife, and a bushy seaman's beard. 'Have ye both travelled far?'

'From Sydney,' Belle said, reaching for another sand-wich. 'We arrived this morning.'

'What brings ye so far from home? Doing a bit of travel-ling?' Mrs Murray asked.

Belle exchanged a look with Riley. 'Actually, we're searching for someone.'

'Och?'

'A man.'

Mrs Murray's cheeks grew pink. 'I'm nae sure you're going to find many single men down this way. Maybe try Edinburgh.'

Riley laughed. 'We're not looking for that kind of man. It's someone we sort of know.'

Mrs Murray released an embarrassed chuckle as Mr Murray shook his head at her. 'Pardon me. In that case, we might be able to help ye. Who is it that you're looking fur?'

'Callum MacKenzie,' Belle said.

Mrs Murray pulled back sharply. 'Callum MacKenzie? *Our* Callum? Just shy of sixty, from Kirkudbright?'

'That sounds about right.'

'Aye, we know him,' Mr Murray said. 'How could we not? Born and bred right here.'

'He's one of our own,' Mrs Murray added.

Belle felt a frisson of energy shoot up her spine. 'So he's here? In the village.'

Mr Murray's face fell. 'No, sorry lassie. He hasn't lived here fur a while. A fine chef he is, though. He moved on some years ago to explore the country and cook.'

'Why is it ye want to find Callum?' Mrs Murray asked.

Belle wasn't sure how much to divulge. Small towns could be rife with big whispers, and it wasn't her intention to set off the rumour mill before she'd had a chance to speak to him. Nevertheless, she was desperate for information, and her head swam with the knowledge that he was no longer there.

'Lass, ye look a bit peely-wally,' Mrs Murray said, sharp eyes assessing her. 'Are ye all right? Best ye take a seat.' She took Belle's elbow and led her to the edge of the bed.

'It's obviously important ye find Callum,' Mr Murray said, watching Belle sit. 'I kin see it on yer face. It's none of our business, of course, but is there a reason fur it? Maybe we kin point ye in the right direction.'

'He knew Belle's mother,' Riley said. 'They became friends while she was travelling through Scotland. We'd like to get in touch with him.'

Belle inhaled shakily, grateful for Riley's intervention and for not divulging the whole truth.

'I see,' Mr Murray said, his eyes still full of questions. But eventually he nodded. 'Well, if it's that important to ye, ye kin try The Selkirk Arms. He used to work there. They might know where he went.'

Belle found her voice. 'Does he still have relatives here?'

'No,' Mr Murray said. 'His parents died several years ago. He has a few siblings, but they're all scattered around Scotland now.'

The disappointment on her face must have been apparent for Mrs Murray patted her arm. 'Why dinnae ye finish yer sandwiches, have a shower and a kip, then we kin walk ye to the Selkirk later. I'm sure Hamish will know where Callum is.'

'Aye, Hamish fur sure.' Mr Murray nodded empathically. 'They were thick as thieves growing up. Best friends.'

'That would be great,' Riley said.

'We'll meet ye downstairs around six,' Mrs Murray said jovially.

They both smiled and left the room, closing the door behind them.

'Uh oh, I can see that look on your face,' Riley said.

Belle's shoulders slumped. 'I knew it would be a stretch, but I'd hoped he would still be here.'

'And yet, that would have been far too easy.'

Belle gave a half-hearted chuckle.

'We're not at a dead end yet,' Riley said, walking to her luggage and unzipping it. 'He might be closer than you think. Let's see what this Hamish guy has to say.'

THE SELKIRK ARMS Hotel was two blocks from Fable House, in the heart of Kirkcudbright. At six sharp, Belle and Riley met the Murrays in their foyer and they walked down together.

Autumn blew a chilly breeze along the high street, fading evening light turning the sky indigo. The terraces they passed along the way had an interesting mix of facades —bursts of pastel-painted render alongside sombre brown brick, next to white pebble dash, with pops of coloured doors. Even if her biological father hadn't once lived there, Belle would still have fallen in love with its Scottish seaside charm.

It took them several minutes to reach the hotel, a large white building with powder blue sills bordering sash and bay windows. They stepped inside to a noisy bar already packed with patrons, walls papered in a deep red and the floor carpeted in tartan. Good old Scottish hospitality was on offer as people greeted the Murrays and invited them to sit at their table.

'Maybe in a bit, Dougal,' Mr Murray said to one man

with a bushy chestnut beard. 'We're looking fur yer cousin Hamish, actually.'

Dougal pointed to a doorway leading to another part of the hotel. 'He's in the other bar. Pop back through later fur a dram.'

'Will do.'

Mrs Murray touched Belle's arm. 'This way, dear. Hamish is in the dining room.'

Belle's palms began to sweat as she and Riley followed the Murrays through the doorway into a packed dining room. Clearly familiar with the hotel, Mr Murray walked directly to a bar in the far corner of the room and leaned against it.

'Hamish,' he said to a ginger-haired man pouring beers behind the bar.

Hamish grinned and thrust out a hand, shaking Mr Murray's, a lock of his carroty hair flopping into his eyes. 'Leith, how are ye doing? Iona.' He nodded at Mrs Murray.

Mrs Murray smiled. 'Hello, Hamish. Keeping well?'

'Aye. As good as kin be.' His eyes fell on Belle and Riley, lingering a second longer on Belle. 'And who dae we have here? Not locals, I'm sure.'

'This is Belle and Riley,' Mrs Murray said. 'They're from Australia.'

'Glad to meet ye.' He finished pouring the beers and set them on a tray, a waitress arriving to whisk them away. 'What kin I get ye all?'

'Nothing fur the moment,' said Mr Murray. 'The lassies here are looking fur Callum MacKenzie. Have ye heard from him lately?'

Hamish's gaze flickered back to Belle. His eyes were so intense on her that her heart began to hammer in her chest. 'Callum?'

'Ye two were always close,' Mrs Murray said. 'We thought ye might keep in touch.'

'Aye, we do,' Hamish said, dropping a dishcloth onto the bar and wiping it down. 'Although we haven't spoken fur a couple of years now. Time just gets away from ye.'

'Aye, it does,' Mr Murray agreed. 'Where was he when ye last spoke to him?'

'Balloch.'

'Where's Balloch?' Belle asked. She had many more burning questions than that—what was he like, did he have a family, children, was he a good person? But it wasn't the time or place to blurt them all out. *Patience*, she told herself. *And breathe!* She was forgetting to breathe.

'It's at the southern end of Loch Lomond,' Mrs Murray explained. 'About an hour north-west of Glasgow.'

'What's he's doing up there?' Mr Murray asked.

'Working in a restaurant. The Stables,' Hamish replied.

'Are ye able to contact him?' Mr Murray persisted. 'Ye could let him know the girls are looking fur him.'

Hamish clicked his tongue. 'I can have a go, but sometimes he's hard to get a hold of. What's the reason you're looking fur him?' His eyes fell directly on Belle again as he asked. 'Fur either I'm needin' glasses or you, lassie, are the spitting image of him.'

Heat rose to Belle's cheeks as Mrs Murray's mouth flopped open. Several seconds passed before she closed it again, wildly fanning herself.

Mr Murray cleared his throat. 'Och, I see. Well, that's uh... that's uh...' He seemed at a loss for words too as he tried not to stare at Belle.

'Are ye staying fur a meal? I'll bring a tray of drinks over,' Hamish offered. He grinned mischievously at them.

'We might as well,' said Mrs Murray, still looking flustered. She turned to the girls. 'They make a mean cock-a-leekie soup here and suddenly I'm needin' to sit down.'

'I'M such a fool fur nae realising Callum was yer da,' Mrs Murray said as they walked back to Fable House after dinner. 'You'd think I would have ken by the look o' ye.'

All through dinner she'd interrogated Belle. When people stopped by their table to talk to the Murrays, she impatiently shooed them away. Between eating and the constant interruptions, Belle could barely get the story out. That was when Mrs Murray insisted her poor husband gulp down his Guinness so they could talk on the way back to Fable House.

'When did ye find out about him?' she asked.

'A few weeks ago,' Belle said. 'My father died in Sydney and my mother told me the truth. So yes, it would appear that Callum MacKenzie is my biological father.'

'I'm sorry fur yer loss, dear,' Mrs Murray said sombrely. 'That must have been a shock to lose yer da, then realise he wasn't yer true da.'

'It was. It is. I'm still processing it.'

'Where did Callum meet yer mother?' Mr Murray asked.

'Here, in Kirkcudbright.'

Mrs Murray glanced at her. 'Your mother was *here*? When?'

'About thirty-eight years ago. She stayed here for two weeks, then they travelled throughout Scotland for two months. Shortly after she arrived back home, she discovered she was pregnant.'

'Ye ken, that's about the time we last saw Callum,' Mrs

Murray said with a pensive expression. 'Am I nae right, Leith?'

Mr Murray nodded thoughtfully. 'Ye could be right, Iona. It has been a while.'

'Aye,' she said, her eyes sparking with recollection. 'In fact, I'm almost certain I remember yer mother passing through. A beautiful young thing, willowy and sweet, and she was Australian if I'm nae mistaken. A bonnie lassie. We dinnae have Fable House at the time, so she dinnae stay with us, but I dae recall now that Callum went travelling with her, although two months later, he returned alone. Shortly after that, looking like his heart had been trampled on by a mob of wild horses, he packed his bags and left again. That was the last time we saw him.'

The wind picked up, gusting down the high street as they walked, the same street her mother and Callum had likely walked once, talking of travel, while they quietly and accidentally fell in love. Then months later, they'd resumed their old lives, but had they ever really moved on?

Belle wondered how often her mother had thought of Callum over the years, how many times Belle had walked into a room and found her staring out the window, lost in memory. Was it Callum and Scotland she'd been remembering? Had she stared at her young daughter and seen, not a mistake as Edward must have seen, but a lost love, turbulent and true?

'How far is Balloch from here?' Riley asked.

'It's about two and a half hours,' Mr Murray said. 'A bonnie spot, well worth the visit even if you're nae searching fur someone.'

'We dae hope you'll stay one more day with us though,' Mrs Murray said, a hopeful expression on her face. 'Kip in tomorrow, then see some of our sights. Explore the village where yer father was raised.'

'Iona's right.' Mr Murray smiled. 'Ye should stay a little longer. It's nice having ye around. Ye *are* Kirkcudbright family, after all.'

NINE

Belle rose early the next morning, jetlag wreaking havoc with her internal clock. The sun was barely up, the room still dark, and she quietly flicked back the covers, careful not to disturb Riley in the next bed.

The air chilled her skin as she walked to the window, parting the curtains slightly to peer outside. The glass was icy, chimney pots and old slate roofs piercing an opaque fog that had settled over the village. Across the shrouded river, mountains rose through the mist and trees were bereft of leaves, autumn stripping them bare. Belle let the curtain fall and returned to her bed.

You are Kirkcudbright family, after all.

The touching sentiment made her smile. The Murrays were lovely people, and she could only hope that some of that warm hospitality would be waiting for her in Balloch when they found Callum.

While she waited for Riley to wake, she checked her phone and saw that Andre had texted her during the middle of the night. He'd apologised for not answering her call the day before but had been busy at work, then had finished late. It was the usual long-distance dance. Even from Scotland, it was difficult.

She glanced at the time on her phone. It was still too early in Rome for her to call—she didn't want to interrupt what little sleep he got—so she replied with another text explaining that they were driving to Balloch, promising to call again soon.

An hour later, Riley rose, and they showered and dressed, meeting Mrs Murray in the dining room for breakfast.

'Come and eat,' she said, pulling out chairs for them. 'I have a nice hot breakfast ready fur ye. Did ye sleep well?'

'Like a log,' Belle said. Riley was beside her, surveying the smorgasbord.

Mrs Murray followed her gaze and beamed. 'Ye must be famished. I made sausages, tatties, bacon, and eggs. And toast!' She fussed over them as they ate, refilling their coffee cups and laying extra condiments and napkins. It was the offseason and as Fable House had no other guests, Belle suspected Mrs Murray had a lot of time on her hands and was enjoying their company.

After breakfast, Belle and Riley helped her clear the dishes away, despite her protests, then returned upstairs to collect their backpacks. Mrs Murray had produced a neatly handwritten list of places she thought they'd like to visit—The Stewartry Museum, the harbour and marina, several boutique art galleries, and the ruins of MacLellan's Castle. She also directed them to the house Callum had grown up in, and it was the first place that Belle dragged Riley.

It was towards the end of the high street, a brown-brick terrace near the castle. As they stood outside, staring up at it, Belle had an overwhelming urge to see inside, to know how Callum had once lived, what kind of child he'd been, the sports he'd liked to play and the hobbies he'd enjoyed. She knew he loved to cook, but what traits did they share beyond that? Did they laugh at the same things, appreciate the same movies? Would he understand her in the way that Edward had struggled to?

'What are you going to say to him when you see him tomorrow?' Riley asked.

They were leaving for Balloch first thing in the morning and it was all she could think about. 'I have no idea. I've turned the moment over in my head so many times it hurts.'

'Start with the truth.'

'I guess I'm worried that the truth will be too difficult. An awful thing was done to him—to us. Time was taken. It can never be restored. How will he deal with that?'

'The same way you dealt with it. With shock and hurt, then with understanding.'

Belle stared up at the narrow terrace windows, the pale sky reflecting in the glass, clouds scudding by. 'What if he's not hurt, just indifferent? What if he has no desire to know me?'

'Then it will be his loss. We'll go home and you won't be left wondering.'

But that was the problem. Even if Callum didn't want to know her, she would always be left wondering. What could have been, what should have been, what would never be. And that was as terrifying as not knowing him at all.

———

ON THE MORNING of their departure to Balloch, they had breakfast at Fable House, settled the bill, then tugged their suitcases to the front door. Mr and Mrs Murray joined them in the foyer, Mrs Murray handing them a small cooler.

'I packed a few things fur yer journey in case ye dinnae want to stop too often. I ken ye must be anxious to get there.' She smiled warmly. 'Just some sandwiches, fruit and homemade shortbread.'

Belle took the cooler from her, placed it on the floor, and gave her a hug. 'Thank you.'

Mrs Murray seemed surprised by the gesture. 'Och my, you're a sweet thing.' She hugged her back, then pulled away, hand on her chest. 'I hope ye find what you're looking fur. I hope ye find Callum.'

'When ye see him, tell him we miss him,' Mr Murray added.

'And drop us a note to let us ken how ye went.'

Belle promised they would, and after Riley hugged Mrs Murray too, they stepped down onto the street and wheeled their suitcases towards the car, Mrs Murray waving to them all the way.

When they reached the car, they stowed their luggage in the boot, and Belle climbed into the driver's seat. Shortly after, they were back on the motorway, heading north towards Balloch. It was a cool day with a cornflower blue sky and a gentle sun that barely warmed the car. The road wended its way through old country villages and farmland, with deep valleys in the distance and castles dotting the hillsides. On any other day, Belle would have given herself up to the beauty of it and suggested places to stop, but Balloch and Callum were close, and she was too jittery to concentrate on anything else.

'Will Andre be flying in?' Riley asked, pulling Mrs Murray's cooler bag onto her lap and unzipping it.

'I hope so. We haven't spoken properly yet. We keep missing each other.'

'The story of your life?'

Belle snorted. 'Exactly.'

'Maybe he can meet us in Balloch.'

'And bring Leo with him.'

Riley frowned at her. 'No, I don't think so.'

'Why not?' Belle asked. Despite the challenges of Riley and Leo's relationship—challenges she knew only too well—she'd always hoped that they'd find a way forward, that Leo's family would accept Riley. Italian culture and tradition were tricky foes to navigate, but their love had been genuine, and Belle didn't want to think that love wasn't enough.

'Because I don't want to see him,' Riley said.

'Have you spoken to him over the last year?'

She pulled an apple out of the cooler, feigning interest in polishing it. 'A message here and there. There hasn't been much to say.'

'He still loves you. Andre told me. Leo always asks him about you.'

'Well, it's a little late for that. We had our chance. It didn't work then and it's not going to work now.' Riley's eyes slid briefly her way. 'What does Andre tell him?'

'What can he tell him? That you went to Perth after Ben's funeral, and we didn't hear from you again. Not even when Andre came to visit.'

This time Riley fixed her with an unyielding stare. 'Well, that's unfair. I didn't exactly hear from you either.'

'But you left. You could have stayed in Sydney.'

'We all cope with trauma in different ways,' she said quietly. 'Like with your nightmares. How long have you been having them?'

Belle squirmed. 'What nightmares?'

'For the past two nights you've been crying out in your

sleep. You've been telling Ben you're sorry. I wasn't going to mention it but if you want to talk, let's talk.'

Belle kept her expression neutral, but her shoulders tensed. 'It's not a big deal. It happens occasionally.'

'Occasionally or always?'

'I said it's not a big deal.' Her nightmares were a coping mechanism, but they were also private and painful and not something she wanted to discuss. If she could bottle up that night in Paris and screw the lid on tightly, locking it away forever, never to be spoken of again, she would.

'I think it's a big deal,' Riley persisted.

'Well, it's not. Are you telling me you've never had a nightmare or two about Paris?'

'Sure, I had them straight after, but I'm not still having them a year later.'

'Oh, you've been left unscathed then?'

Riley gave a derisive snort. 'Unscathed? Hardly. No one could walk away from a night like that unscathed. I struggle in crowds, I'm unsettled and yes, I think about what happened *all* the time. I think about Ben and Avery and the bomb. My ears still ring and my head aches and my heart races in my chest, but I've been talking to someone—a therapist—and it's helping. Not a lot, but a little. Your problem is that you won't talk to anyone.'

'I'm still grieving,' she said. Her hands grew clammy on the wheel.

'No, you have survivor's guilt and it's unnecessary,' Riley said. 'You weren't to blame for what happened.'

Belle blinked back a surge of hot tears. She wasn't sure why she wouldn't bite the bullet and see a professional, someone who could help her unpack the complex layers of emotions she felt, except that talking was hard. Internalising was easier. Ignoring, disbelieving, denying meant, in some way, she could forget. But was she really forgetting?

'Your mum's concerned about you,' Riley said. 'She thinks you're not coping.'

'How would she know? She's seen me a handful of times in the last year.'

'Exactly! The fact that you're avoiding her tells her you're not okay.' Her voice was firm. 'You weren't the reason Ben was in Paris and you're not the reason he died.'

'Just like I'm not the reason Avery was there, or Andre?' Belle's bottom lip quivered. Her chest tightened, stealing her breath. A moment later, she felt Riley's hand on her shoulder, and she took an almighty breath, filling her lungs with a rattling sob, letting the tears scurry down her cheeks.

'You should pull over,' Riley said softly. 'You can't drive like this.'

'I'm okay,' she said, wiping her face and pulling herself together.

Riley sighed deeply. 'Sorry. I didn't mean to upset you. But I love you and I'm worried.'

Belle glanced at her with a watery smile. 'And I'm worried about you too. Like you said, we all cope in our own way.'

'Let's just not be so alone anymore,' Riley said. 'And no more guilt. You couldn't have prevented Paris any more than I could have.'

Belle gave an infinitesimal nod and made a solemn, silent promise to do better, to open up more, to not swaddle her trauma so close. It was easier said than done. Giving voice to that night made it real. Perhaps that was what she hadn't come to terms with yet. That Ben and Avery were gone. That she'd almost lost Riley and Andre. That life was as fragile as eggshells sometimes because an entirely different set of decisions would mean that Ben and Avery could still be alive.

A sign for Glasgow appeared and the GPS on her phone indicated that Balloch was forty minutes away. She steeled herself, pushing thoughts of Paris aside. Soon she would have other things to worry about, like meeting her biological father for the first time and how she was going to explain *that* to him.

TEN

After navigating through Glasgow's frenetic streets, the signs to Balloch and Loch Lomond appeared and Belle's trepidation intensified. Butterflies had been a constant companion on the drive, but they caused a riot now in her stomach.

The jungle of city housing eventually relented to woodlands of Scots pine and oak, and cotton wool clouds gathered over small hillside towns. The moment they entered Balloch, Belle's brain began tossing out all the reasons why tracking her father down wasn't a good idea— he was happily married, surrounded by children and grand-children, with no desire to want to know her. Blood pulsed in her temples, a stress headache looming. *What am I doing?*

They negotiated surprisingly energetic streets where tourists still lingered and probably always would this close to winter and the Highlands. They turned at an intersection and reached the carpark of the establishment Hamish had told them Callum worked at—The Stables.

'Should we check into a hotel first?' Riley asked as Belle

parked the car. 'It's just after lunch. If he's not working until dinner, we'll have to wait.'

'Let's try first. If he's not here, we'll find a hotel and come back later.' She had to push forward or her nerve would collapse.

They climbed out of the car, the cold like a slap to Belle's cheeks. She wrapped her scarf around her neck as Riley tugged on a beanie, and they walked to the front door. Once inside, they strode towards the first bar they saw and were greeted by the bartender.

'What kin I get ye?' he asked, wiping beer glasses and stacking them on a rack.

'Hi,' Belle said, certain he could hear her heart smashing against her ribcage. 'We're looking for someone who works here.'

'Och?' He was young with a boyish grin and playful eyes framed by long lashes. 'Who's the lucky person then?' His gaze fell on Riley and she boldly held it, smiling.

'Callum MacKenzie,' Belle said. 'Do you know him?'

'The chef? Aye, I know Callum.'

Hope collided with her anxiety. 'You do?'

'Aye, but he doesnae work here anymore. He left about a year ago.'

The hope collapsed and she wilted with disappointment. 'You're kidding?'

The bartender shrugged hesitantly. 'Sorry, he moved on.'

'Is he still in the area?'

The guy placed the glass he was wiping down. 'He used to live up by Loch Lomond, but as far as I know, he went further north. I'm nae sure where to.'

Belle slumped against the bar, deflated. She'd pinned all her hopes on finding him in Balloch and her heart plummeted with the realisation that not only had he moved on, he'd done so a year ago. Which meant he could be anywhere by now.

The bartender smiled sympathetically at her. 'If it helps, I kin ask the head chef where he went. He might know.'

'Please,' Riley said.

Belle waited until the bartender had disappeared through a doorway, presumably into the kitchen, before she spoke. 'He's not here.'

'Just a small setback,' Riley said quickly.

'I'd mentally prepared myself,' Belle lamented. 'I even had my opening line ready.' It had been an awkward explanation that she'd crafted the night before while lying awake staring at the ceiling but still, she'd been ready.

'If he left here a year ago, he's probably still at the next place. No one moves around *that* much.'

'What if we don't know where that next place is?'

'Stop panicking,' Riley hissed. 'You're making me anxious.'

The bartender returned followed by a short, rotund man in chef's whites with a dishtowel slung over his shoulder. 'This is Gilroy, the head chef.'

'Why are ye looking fur Callum?' Gilroy demanded. He looked harried and annoyed, as though they'd interrupted him.

'We need to find him,' Belle explained.

'Aye, but *why*?' Gilroy repeated. 'I'm nae in the habit of giving out people's private information to strangers.'

'It's... complicated,' Belle said.

'This is his daughter,' Riley blurted out. 'Is that a good enough reason for you?'

Belle frowned at her. So much for telling Callum first. Half of Scotland would know before he did.

Gilroy leaned in closely, studying her features, until finally, he straightened. 'Well, now that ye mention it, ye dae look a lot like him. Ye have his eyes.'

'So you'll tell us where he went?' Riley persisted.

Gilroy sighed heavily. 'I'm still nae one fur giving out people's information, but I kin tell ye that he moved to Dundee. Broughty Ferry, to be exact.'

'Where's that?' Belle asked.

'On the east coast of Scotland,' the bartender said. 'About a two-hour drive north-east from here.'

'And do you know where he's working now?'

'Nae where he's working,' Gilroy said, 'but he did have me mail him some documents after he left. I dinnae ken if that's where he's living now. I think it was just a forwarding address until he got settled. I won't give out his phone number, but I suppose I could give ye that address. It'll send ye in the right direction, at least.'

Belle almost threw her arms around him.

'In the meantime, I'll try and call him, let him ken that you're looking fur him. Although he kin be a bit hard to reach sometimes.'

'Thank you, Gilroy,' Belle said. 'If you do get a hold of him, please don't tell him...'

'That you're his daughter?' Gilroy smiled softly. 'Lass, in all the years I've worked with Callum, he's never once mentioned having a bairn. This is going to be a shock fur him. Dinnae worry, I'll let ye break the news.'

'Thank you.'

He fished out a pen from his chef's jacket, wrote the Broughty Ferry address on the back of a coaster and handed it to her. In turn, she wrote her mobile number on another coaster for him. 'In case you speak to Callum and he wants to contact me,' she said.

Gilroy glanced at her number, then nodded and placed the coaster in his jacket pocket. 'Good luck with yer search, lassie. Callum's a good man. I hope ye find what you're looking fur.' He strode back into the kitchen.

The bartender gave Riley a disappointed look. 'I guess that means you'll be heading straight to Broughty Ferry then.'

'We don't want to risk losing him,' Riley said, looking equally as disappointed.

'Maybe I should give ye my number in case ye have more questions.' His expression was hopeful.

Riley whipped her phone out so swiftly she knocked Belle on the shoulder. 'Good idea!'

They exchanged numbers, the bartender unable to wipe the smile from his face. 'I'm Quinn.'

'Riley.'

'And I'm Belle.' But neither of them seemed to hear her.

They exited the restaurant and returned to the car, Riley grinning all the way.

'Made a friend, did you?' Belle teased.

She pressed the car remote to unlock the doors, still smiling like a Cheshire cat. 'I've forgotten how good it feels to flirt. I guess it's been a quiet year.'

Belle's heart tugged. Riley was too beautiful for quiet years and although she claimed to be coping after Paris, maybe she felt the aftershocks too, in ways that weren't as obvious as nightmares or denial.

For the journey to Broughty Ferry, Riley took over the driving, steering them out of Balloch so Belle could call Andre.

'Have you got a few minutes to talk?' she asked when he

answered. It was the middle of the lunch shift at Valentina's and it sounded busy.

'Sure, just a second.' He asked someone to watch the bar, then the background noise faded as she heard him move through the front door and out into the laneway. 'That's better. How are you?'

'Good. I'm sorry we missed each other's calls.'

'*Bella,* don't ever apologise. It can't be helped.' She heard scraping and could see him pulling a chair out to sit, the steel legs catching the old cobbles. 'Where are you now?'

'We're leaving Balloch.'

'Did you find Callum?'

'He wasn't there. He relocated to Broughty Ferry a year ago.'

'Oh no! What are you going to do now?' he asked.

'We're heading to Broughty. Do you think you could meet us?' She held her breath, hoping for a yes, but prepared for a no. Even in the offseason, Valentina's flourished, and it was unreasonable to expect he could get time away.

'I'll check with my father,' Andre said. 'A couple of days shouldn't hurt. I could fly out tomorrow morning.'

Belle's smile grew wide. The uncertainty of finding Callum had made her long for Andre's steadiness, the quiet force of his presence, and she was already counting down the hours until he arrived. 'You can fly into Glasgow and drive up to Dundee.'

'Send me your hotel details once you check in. I'll meet you there.'

'Be safe, my love.'

'*Ti amo.*'

They ended the call and Belle dropped her phone into her bag.

'So he's coming?' Riley asked.

'Yes. Tomorrow. He'll meet us at the hotel.' Balloch was quickly retreating behind them and they were cast back out onto the open road, flat planes and grassy hillsides gracing the landscape.

'It's still hard to believe we're here,' Belle said, staring out the window.

'It was a brave move, kid, but the right one.'

'You think so?'

Riley nodded. 'I know so. You're not just an Australian anymore. You belong to Scotland now too. This is where you need to search for him, not on the internet.'

The journey to Scotland had always been about finding Callum, but she hadn't paused to consider that Scotland was also about *her*. Her heritage and parentage, her ancestors and their stories, the bloodlines and family tree, branches extending that she never knew existed before, reaching out to new possibilities. She was learning more about herself and Callum than she could ever have hoped to learn on a website and although everything felt uncertain, maybe Riley was right. This was where she needed to be.

'I have a good feeling about Broughty Ferry,' Riley said.

'Me too,' Belle agreed. 'I desperately want him to be there.'

'He will be.'

Belle played with a loose thread on her jeans, a question on the tip of her tongue that had been plaguing her for days. 'Do you think my dad would have wanted this? Edward, I mean.'

Riley didn't answer straight away, but when she did, it

was with conviction. 'Yes. I would even go as far as to say that he would have told you himself eventually.'

'Really?'

'Absolutely. Why do you think your mum told you?'

'Because I dragged it out of her,' Belle said wryly.

'Maybe. But in the end, she told you what you needed to know. Secrets become heavy over time, especially when someone hauls them around for decades. You're not betraying your dad. I think he would have been happy for you to know because trying to make you someone you weren't was painful for him too.'

'Then why did he do it?'

'He wanted you to be his.'

While Riley's words gave her some comfort, it was difficult to completely shake the worry that coiled inside her—that of finding Callum and being welcomed into his world and the guilt over betraying her late father's memory. It was coupled always with the constant unease about Andre and the future, about Ben and Avery and Paris. And whether the girl she used to be was lost forever.

ELEVEN

Dundee was one of Scotland's sunniest locations, sprawled along the northern shore of the Firth of Tay, as a barista happily informed them when they stopped for coffee just outside the city.

While he made their coffees, Belle showed him the back of the coaster with the address that Gilroy had written down and he nodded with approval.

'Aye, Broughty Ferry. About twenty miles from here. A very nice place, right on the sea.'

'And Brook Street?'

'About three blocks back from the water. Also very nice.'

Belle thanked him for the information, paid for the coffees, and left the café with Riley, walking back out to the car.

'What's the plan?' Riley asked, leaning against the driver's door, and taking a sip from her cup.

'Let's go straight to Brook Street.'

'And what if Callum's not there? Remember what Gilroy said. It's probably only a forwarding address.'

'Or it might be where he lives. At the least, I'm hoping someone there will know where we can find him.'

'It's getting late,' Riley said, squinting up at the languishing sun. 'We should find a hotel. I don't want to sleep in this car.'

'I promise we'll check into one straight after,' Belle said, opening the passenger door and climbing in.

Riley navigated them back onto the road and they drove the remaining distance to Dundee, following the coastal route into Broughty Ferry. The GPS guided them onto Brook Street, and Riley found a parking spot three doors down from the house number Gilroy had written on the coaster.

They climbed out of the car, Belle glancing up and down the street. It was picturesque, with quaint fisherman cottages and Victorian terraces threaded amongst bars and restaurants. It bustled with charm and personality and boutique independent stores that coloured the town.

Riley locked the doors and they followed the row of terraces until they were standing outside the house, a neat brown-brick Victorian with white brickwork trim and single-pane sash windows. The front garden was framed by a low garden wall with a black gate.

'Should we knock?' Riley asked.

'I guess,' Belle said. The small amount of confidence she'd assembled on the drive from Balloch slowly wilted, and the traitorous butterflies returned to steal her nerve. What if it wasn't a forwarding address and Callum answered? Should she deliver the news swiftly or break it to him gently? What if his wife answered and demanded to know who they were? Gilroy had confirmed that Callum hadn't fathered other children, but he hadn't said anything about a wife.

She pushed through the black gate and stepped up onto the small porch, giving the front door a tentative knock. After a minute of waiting, Riley pressed her ear to the door and shrugged. Belle knocked again, but there was still no answer.

'No one's home,' Riley said.

Belle slumped, her spirits flagging. 'Maybe we should wait in the car. Whoever lives here might be back soon. *He* might be back soon.'

'Or he could be out for hours, especially if he's working in a kitchen.' Riley touched her arm. 'It's getting late. We need to find a place to stay.'

Belle stared out across the rooftops as the sun dragged the last of the daylight away. Riley was right. They'd been driving all day and were exhausted. They couldn't risk spending the night in the car. It was almost six pm, and the air was growing colder, nightfall coming fast. 'All right, let's go. We can come back tomorrow.'

THEY CHECKED into a hotel a short walk from the beach and Riley took a shower while Belle called her mother. Despite some texts, Belle hadn't yet filled her in on their progress with finding Callum, what little there was of it.

'You're where?' Grace asked when Belle phoned her.

'Broughty Ferry, near Dundee.'

'Oh, yes,' she replied, nostalgia in her voice. 'Callum and I went there. We stayed in a little place by the beach. It's a lovely town.'

'We followed him here from Balloch,' Belle said.

'Now that brings back memories. We visited there too. Spent a few nights camping on Loch Lomond.'

'He seems to work his way around the kitchens in Scotland. He was in Balloch for a couple of years and we're hoping we've caught up with him here in Broughty. We have an address.' She told her mother about the terrace on Brook Street. 'Does it mean anything to you?'

'No, sorry, sweetheart. Like I said, we were only there a short while.'

'Tell me about him, Mum. Who's the man I'm chasing?'

She steeled herself for her mother's resistance, but there was a soft, almost capitulating sigh on the other end. 'He was a lovely man when I knew him, thoughtful and funny. People were drawn to him. He could make you feel like you were the only person in the room. And the way he cooked, with such passion... I see that in you. That intensity for creation and food.'

'I want to find him,' Belle said with renewed determination.

'I know, sweetheart. I just hope it's not too much of a shock for him.'

'I heard from someone that he doesn't have other children.'

'Did he ever marry?'

'I don't know.' She wished she'd thought to ask Hamish or Gilroy.

'Did you start in Kirkcudbright?'

Belle smiled. 'Yes. We stayed with the Murrays at Fable House, and we met Callum's best friend Hamish.'

'Oh yes,' Grace said. 'I remember Hamish. A cheeky fellow. Just like your father. I mean, you know... Callum.'

'It's okay. I do it too. Sometimes I forget and call him my father and other times, I don't know what to call Dad. I feel guilty, as though I'm letting them both down.'

'Edward will always be your father,' Grace said. 'You can call Callum whatever feels right.'

'For now, it should just be Callum. I don't know him. I'm not even sure I'm going to find him.'

'For what it's worth, I hope you do. I know I resisted at the start. I was afraid of what he'd think of me once you told him the truth. I still do, but you need him and I'm sure he needs you.'

'Do you really think so?' The words were soothing, and she let them wrap around her.

'Yes, I do.'

To finally have her mother's support dispelled some of the angst. It was one less thing she had to worry about. 'How are you going back there?'

Grace sighed. 'Still adjusting. I pottered around in your father's office today, just looking. I'm not sure I can pack it away yet.'

'Then don't. It's too soon.'

'Yes, it is too soon,' she said tiredly. 'You think you have time with someone—time to apologise, to explain, to tell them that you *did* love them, until suddenly that time runs out and all you're left with is emptiness because those opportunities died with them.'

'Dad knew you loved him and that you were sorry for what you did,' Belle said. 'You can't keep punishing yourself for the past.'

'Maybe. But it's not just him that I need to apologise to. It's to you and Callum as well. I took a lot away from you both. Loyalty to your father and all those years I spent trying to atone for my mistakes cost everyone more than it should have. I didn't know who I was back then, and I don't know who I am now.'

'Mum...' Belle could hear her mother's exhaustion, her

grief and anguish spilling over. She would have done anything to reach across the continents and hug her, to tell her that she didn't blame her. 'We're going to set things right, you and me, okay?'

'You're the one setting things right, and you're very brave for doing it.'

'Let's see how brave I am when I come face to face with him,' Belle said.

After a few more minutes, they ended the call, but Belle's heart was weighted again with a sorrow she couldn't explain. Her mother despaired and it did little to quell the apprehension she felt. At times she was elated to be in Scotland, seeking out her father, at others, she was a bundle of nerves. And the next day, there was every chance she would meet Callum, which both excited and terrified her.

The shower turned off and the glass shower door squeaked open. She needed a shower too, to let the hot water soak into her muscles and the steam clear her head, followed by a warm meal and hopefully a restful night's sleep. Then, in the morning, with a little luck, someone would answer the door on Brook Street.

———————

BELLE ROSE EARLY the next morning and let herself out onto the small balcony while she waited for Riley to wake. The morning was cold, a half-hearted sun rising and the sky shifting and sighing while it found daylight. Pale rays rippled across the River Tay as it marched towards the firth, casting out into the North Sea. The same fingers of light draped across the grey stone of Broughty Castle, cutting a dignified figure by the water's edge.

Was Callum watching this sunrise, the same soft light

that tiptoed across the bay? Or was he asleep, exhausted after a night of working in a kitchen not far from where she was? The thought of him being so close caused trepidation to slip under her skin again.

She tugged her coat around her pyjamas, scrunching her toes together against the chill as she heard covers rustling and Riley yawn. She cast one last look at the water, then walked back inside to get dressed.

Down at breakfast, Riley buttered a piece of toast and took a bite. 'Sleep well?' she asked around a mouthful.

'Not really,' Belle said, sipping espresso.

'We should go find Callum after eating,' Riley said. 'Put you out of your misery.'

Belle agreed. She wasn't about to torture herself any longer by dragging her heels.

They finished breakfast and rather than taking the car, they walked the short distance to Brook Street. The morning had warmed slightly, the sun mild as they strolled through the town. Neat rows of villas and terraces lined the streets, interspersed by boutique shops and arty cafés. But it was the restaurants that caught Belle's eye. She held the gaze of every man who stepped in and out of them, expecting to glimpse Callum. She hadn't the faintest clue what he looked like, only had her features to gauge from, but she hoped that in her heart she would know who he was the minute she set eyes on him.

When they arrived on Brook Street and stood before the house once again, Belle lifted her chin and pushed through the black gate. She gave the door a solid knock and waited.

'I hope we're not too early,' she said, glancing at her watch. It was just on nine.

Determined high heels echoed down the hall, then the door opened to a petite woman with thick, glossy brown hair and bright red lips. Voluptuous cleavage spilled from a yellow tank top and a tight black mini skirt hugged slim hips. 'Yes?' she asked in a sultry Spanish accent.

'Hi,' Belle said. 'We're sorry to disturb you. We're looking for someone who might have lived here once.'

'Who?' she asked, thick-lashed eyes narrowing.

'Callum MacKenzie.'

The woman scoffed. 'You *know* Callum MacKenzie?' Her suspicious gaze swept over them both before she launched into a tirade. '*Esa bastardo!* So now he's replaced me with someone younger. And not just one woman, but two!' Spanish expletives began flying from her lips, eyes fiery, her arms waving about. 'Is this the game he wants to play? Well he can go to hell. *Tonto del culo!*'

Belle opened her mouth to explain but the woman held up her hand.

'What did he do? Break your heart too? Tell you he loved you then he left?'

'No,' Belle said, glancing at Riley, who was staring transfixed at the woman.

'When you find him, tell him I never want to see him again. Slap him in the face for me!' She folded her arms across her breasts. 'You tell him, from Carlota, that we could have had a good life together. He will come back one day, begging for forgiveness, and I will be gone.' She let out a furious huff. 'Gone!'

Belle swallowed. 'We... uh.' She couldn't find her words in the face of all that fury.

Thankfully Riley had words. 'Do you know where we can find him?'

'No, I do not,' Carlota said, her arms still crossed, her pout full. After a few seconds, her shoulders relaxed. 'Well, maybe I heard from a friend that he headed west.'

'You mean he's not here anymore?' Belle squeaked.

'In Broughty Ferry? No. He left four months ago. One morning he packed his bags, told me he was sorry and left. You can't hang onto Callum MacKenzie for long. Don't even try.' She wagged her finger at them.

'Do you know the name of the town he went to?' Riley asked.

'Someone said Fort William, in the West Highlands.'

'Why did he leave?' Riley persisted.

'How should I know? One minute we were fine and the next, I mentioned babies, and he left.'

Belle's nerves jangled and not just because he was no longer there. *I mentioned babies, and he left.*

'Thank you,' Riley said. 'And we're sorry he broke your heart.'

Carlota's pride flared across her face and she jutted out her chin. 'Someone must have broken his long ago because he's impossible to get close to. Good luck with that!'

Belle gave her a sad smile and turned to leave.

'Wait.' Carlota reached for her arm, her expression tender suddenly. 'If you find him, tell him...' she sighed dolefully, 'tell him I am still here.' She nodded, then closed the door.

TWELVE

The walk back to the hotel was heavy with silence, Belle turning Carlota's words over in her head. *I mentioned babies, and he left.* Six little words that had completely thrown her.

Riley seemed to sense the reason for the disquiet and cleared her throat. 'Just because he didn't want babies with Carlota doesn't mean he never wanted them in the first place.'

'He left her because she asked to start a family,' Belle argued.

'Carlota's young, easily half Callum's age. We know he's older. Maybe he didn't want children at this stage of his life. Maybe he didn't want them with *her*.'

'But he's never had them. Gilroy confirmed that.'

'Again, it doesn't mean he *never* wanted them. Maybe he never found the right person to settle down with.'

There was logic in her words, but Belle couldn't shake the feeling that Callum had inadvertently revealed an important part of himself. His lack of children might have been a conscious choice. He'd *chosen* not to have them, just like he'd chosen to run the moment Carlota had suggested it. None of that boded well for Belle if she was expecting anything from her biological father.

'Don't be discouraged by this,' Riley said. 'This has nothing to do with you.'

'Or maybe it has everything to do with me. Maybe Mum knew that Callum wouldn't support her if she told him about the pregnancy.'

'We don't know that. You're jumping the gun.'

But it was impossible not to. By the time they reached the hotel lobby, the horse had already bolted and her fears along with it. Tracking Callum down had been premature and naïve. She'd known nothing about this man, had dived in blindly, and the more he revealed to her, the more she realised this was probably destined to end in heartbreak.

As they crossed the polished tiles, out of the corner of her eye, she saw a figure rise from a chair and walk towards her. It took her less than a second to realise who it was—tall with dark hair and an angular face she knew well. And that presence. That undeniably solid presence.

Andre.

She ran to him and he swept her up in his arms, holding her so tight, fingers bunched in her hair, that her breath left her. Her disappointment over Callum, along with Paris, her father's death and the last year fell away, eclipsed by the moment.

'You're here,' she whispered into his neck. He smelled of everything she remembered about him, soap and bergamot and a hint of espresso. The last time she'd seen him had been six months ago when she'd met him in Prague, and their days together had been too brief.

'I came straight from the airport,' he said, pulling back

to look at her with concern, brushing her cheek with his fingertips. 'You're unhappy. What's happened?'

'Callum,' she said. 'He's not here.'

'But I thought...'

She shook her head. 'He left.'

'How long ago?'

'Four months.'

Riley joined them and Andre dragged his arms and gaze away from Belle to embrace her. 'Riley, it's been too long.'

'The last time I saw you was in Paris, and you didn't look too great.' Although her tone was light, her eyes grew uncharacteristically shiny, and she turned away from him.

'I wasn't, but because of you, I was lucky. I never did get to thank you for saving me.'

For a sobering moment, their gazes met, silent words of understanding and gratitude passing between them.

'Anyway, tell me what happened with Callum. Are we too late?' He tucked Belle's hand in his, collected his duffel bag from the chair, and they walked to the elevator.

Belle pressed the button. 'We visited an address where we thought he might be. Turns out, his jilted lover was there instead, a very fiery lady who's still nursing a broken heart over him.'

'And where has Callum gone?'

'To Fort William apparently,' Riley said. 'West Scotland.'

'But we have no address or workplace to start with,' Belle added, as the elevator doors chimed open and they stepped inside. 'If we went there, we'd be cold searching.'

'How big is Fort William?' Andre asked.

'I'm not sure.'

The doors opened on their floor, and they stepped out. Andre hadn't let go of Belle's hand since the lobby and didn't take his eyes off her now as they walked down the corridor. Riley pulled the room card from her pocket and inserted it, pushing through the door.

They walked into the room and Andre dropped his bag onto an armchair.

'How was the flight?' Belle asked. There were so many other things she wanted to say to him that asking about his flight seemed inconsequential.

'It was good.'

'How long can you stay?'

'A few days. Then I'll need to get back.'

While Riley disappeared into the bathroom, Belle took Andre outside to show him the view from the balcony. Out there, overlooking the water, he held her close, arms circled tightly around her waist. They didn't speak, just held tight to each other. She wondered how she'd existed without him for all those months, how she would exist again once he left. For the next few days her world would be full, then he would leave and it would be empty, and she hated that part of their relationship—the excitement of seeing each other always overshadowed by the agonising farewell that would follow.

They left the balcony and stepped back into the room to find Riley standing by the door, car keys in one hand and a backpack in the other.

'Where are you going?' Belle asked.

Riley flicked her hair off her shoulder and swung her backpack onto it. 'I figured you might like some time together.'

'You don't have to leave,' Andre said. 'I was planning to get my own room.'

Riley held up the car keys. 'It's not necessary. I'm

driving back to Balloch. There's a certain bartender there who's expecting me.'

'You're going to drive all the way back to Balloch?' Belle's guilt was immediate. Riley had accompanied her on this journey. She didn't want her to feel like the third wheel.

'I am. Quinn invited me, and I accepted.' She put her arms around Belle and hugged her. 'You guys need this. And I need it too.'

'But...' Belle leaned back to study Riley's face for any sign she might feel unwanted. 'Are you sure?'

Riley's smile was genuine. 'Positive. I'll meet you in Fort William in a couple of days.'

'I'm not sure I'll be going,' Belle said.

Riley gave her a disapproving look. 'Yes, you will. Don't let what Carlota said about babies discourage you.'

'What about babies?' Andre asked.

Belle frowned. 'It's a long story. And it's not just about that,' she said. 'It's all of it.'

'I've never known you to give up, kid,' Riley chastised. 'Don't start now. What were your words to me before we came here? You'll turn this place upside down if you have to?'

Belle broke into a reluctant smile. 'Okay, I might have said that.'

'You did. I have a good memory.' She patted Belle's arm. 'Forget about Callum for now. Enjoy your time together. And I'll see you both in Fort William.'

Before Belle could protest again, she waved goodbye to them and left the room.

As soon as the door clicked shut, Andre wasted no time crossing the floor in two strides to reach her, pulling her into him, crushing his mouth down on hers. All the longing and loneliness and distance they'd endured was in that kiss, frenzied and furious, as though they couldn't get enough of each other. His hands were in her hair, his body pressed against her, and she could feel him strong and wanting.

Then Andre slowed and he drew a shaky breath. 'God, I've missed you, but I don't want to rush this.'

Belle's breath was ragged too, her heart crashing against her ribs.

He dropped his forehead to hers, their eyelashes touching. 'I want to undress you slowly, to look at you and taste you and I want to take my time, even if all I want to do right now is rip your clothes off.'

He held her gaze as she flicked the buttons of his shirt open and he tugged her jumper over her head, her hair slipping free, falling around her bare shoulders. She no longer wore braids because she wasn't that innocent girl-next-door anymore, the kind who didn't know how cruel the world could be. He cupped her face in his hands and stroked her cheeks with his thumbs, her eyes fluttering closed. For so long he'd only existed in her dreams, months of wishing him close when he was so far away, and now he *was* here, *was* touching her.

He bent to kiss her, softly, slowly—her eyelids, the tip of her nose, the corners of her mouth, then her lips as she parted them and let his tongue find hers. His lips drifted slowly across her chin, down to her neck, dragging them along her throat, as her head fell back, exposing her skin to him. He unhooked her bra and let it drop, fingers tracing her shoulders, her collarbone, then down to her breasts.

'You are so beautiful,' he murmured. Then his lips found hers again, and for all their intended restraint, the hunger returned and he kissed her, his tongue seeking and teasing, filling her with a warmth that crooned. He picked her up in one deft move, carried her to the bed and laid her down, tugging her jeans and underwear off and climbing out of his.

Desire tore through her, blocking out the world. Her problems would be waiting for her tomorrow, but for now, they'd been silenced. Her skin was humming and prickling, her soul crying out for permeance, heat spreading through her. Nothing had ever or would ever feel as complete as his strong, lean body on hers. She pulled him down on top of her, wrapping her arms and legs around him, the long line of his back hard and smooth as his kisses, sometimes urgent, sometimes feather-light, explored her body.

The foreplay was exquisite, but neither of them was able to resist any longer as she moaned his name and he responded, rocking into her like the waves of the oceans that kept them apart.

And she knew that, just like her, he was lost to the same earth-shattering oblivion, where time became liquid, and distance and obligations were, for the moment, subdued.

THIRTEEN

Belle awoke to the sun setting behind Broughty Ferry, shadows gathering on the walls in soft grey light. She and Andre had eventually fallen asleep, satiated, months of absent time recovered, moments lost and found.

She rolled over, her fingers creeping across the sheets until she found him. He was still sleeping, lying on his back, one arm raised above his head. He was beautiful and masculine, long dark lashes framing closed eyes, and a faint shadow of stubble that had grazed her skin pleasantly as he'd kissed her all afternoon. His lips were full, so perfect to kiss, and she still loved the deep dimples that hollowed his cheeks. He had a defined chest and stomach with delicious V-lines that ran down his hips and, beneath the covers, legs that were sculptured from walking across Rome every day.

Oh, how she'd missed him. His body, his mind, that prepossessing smile that coaxed and caressed her. She'd missed their time together, something that could easily be taken for granted were it not such a privilege.

Andre stirred and opened his eyes. He smiled lazily,

then stretched and rolled over to face her. 'How long have we been asleep for?'

'I'm not sure,' she said, creeping closer to him, as he draped his arm over her. 'It's late afternoon.'

'An espresso would be nice.'

'Shall I order some up?' she asked, rising onto her elbow.

He stared at her, his gaze sweeping over her body before pulling her back down again. 'Not just yet. I want to enjoy you a little more first.'

She laughed and let him wrap himself around her. His arms were tanned from the Mediterranean sun, lean and firm from hauling boxes and crates of produce into Valentina's. She studied the burn scar stamped on his right bicep, then traced her finger along a scar at his temple and the corresponding divot on his jawline where shrapnel had embedded itself.

She would never forget the moment she'd seen him lying in the hospital bed in Paris, battered and broken, thinking she had lost him forever. Not just to his injuries, but to expectation, to Mary, Rome, and culture. The thought made her pull him a little closer and he seemed to understand without her voicing it, tightening his arms around her.

'I can't believe we get to spend the next three days together,' she said, still marvelling at the unexpected gift.

'It was a nice thing that Riley did.'

'She hasn't done much living lately. She needed this too.'

'And you?' he asked. 'Have you been living?'

She picked at a loose thread of cotton on the sheet's seam to avoid his eyes. 'I'm fine.'

'Belle...'

They fell silent, but the quiet was anything but peaceful. 'It hasn't been a walk in the park, if that's what you're asking,' she admitted.

'No, it hasn't,' he said, 'but it *has* been a year. And you're still struggling.'

His gaze was steady on her, and she still found it disarming—his ability to see inside her soul and witness her deepest vulnerabilities. 'How does one move on completely after what we went through?' she asked. 'How does one close their eyes and not see their dead friends' faces?' She didn't wait for an answer, and he didn't offer one. She rolled onto her back and stared at the AC duct in the ceiling above, avoiding his penetrating stare.

'I'm worried you're not sleeping.'

'I do sleep, sometimes,' she said. 'But when I do, I dream. And when I try to sleep lightly instead, I wake exhausted. I don't know how to stop the cycle.' She fixed him with a doleful expression. 'How do you do it—be okay with it all? What's the magic formula?'

'There is no magic formula and I'm not okay with it,' he said, defensiveness creeping into his voice. 'I struggle too. I grieve for my cousin, who shouldn't have died that night. I grieve for us because we can't be together and yes, I grieve for Ben because losing him still hurts you. Don't tell me I'm okay with it. But at some point, we must keep moving forward, or we'll get stuck. We didn't die. We're still alive, so we need to *live*.'

Belle blinked her tears away, turning back to the duct in the ceiling. 'Let's talk about something else.'

'The problem is you don't talk enough.'

'I don't want to spend our three days together talking about *this*. Please?'

He was still staring at her in that inscrutable way that

meant he wasn't happy dropping the topic, but Paris was Paris and no amount of talking would change any of it. He'd witnessed her nightmares when he'd visited her in Sydney, had seen how reduced her life had become. And while she'd seen him jump at sudden noises too, watched him break a sweat in a crowd, heard his voice grow sad whenever they spoke of Avery, he was moving forward, just like Riley. Just like everyone around her while her feet remained firmly planted on those cobbled streets in Paris.

'How's Valentina's?' she asked, turning back towards him, keen to change the subject.

He sighed with resignation. 'It's fine. Busy, but good.'

'And your father. How is the new sous chef doing?'

'He quit.'

'But that's three sous chefs in the past year!'

'We'll find a replacement soon. The problem is we no longer have an arrangement with immigration officials to hire foreigners, so we need to offer competitive wages. We employ and train staff, then they move on to other restaurants who offer better salaries, the ones along the piazzas who get the lion's share of the tourists.' He stroked her cheek. 'And my father hasn't found anyone like you. You always understood him in the kitchen. At times, I think he'd rather cook alone than have someone other than you.'

'And yet, he was so desperate to get rid of me.' She remembered his words in the hospital when she'd gone to see Andre and had been encouraged to say goodbye instead.

'Ah, they are not the same thing. As a chef, he highly respects you. He would prefer to work with you over anyone else in Rome.'

'But as a daughter-in-law?'

Andre shrugged solemnly. 'That's a little more complicated.'

When it came to Andre and Mary and being Italian, it always was. 'Does he still hope that one day you'll marry Mary?'

'Sometimes. Although I think mostly he's given up.'

'And Mary, has *she* given up?'

Andre cast her a sharp look. 'What's that supposed to mean?'

'Exactly what it sounds like. Do you spend time with her?'

Andre hauled himself into a sitting position. 'Are you picking a fight with me?'

'No. I'm just asking if you and Mary spend time together.'

'What you're really asking is if I've been intimate with her.'

That was exactly what she was asking and although he was clearly infuriated by the question, she couldn't stop herself. 'Fine, that's what I'm asking. Mary's right there, in Rome, every day. And I'm not.'

'So you think that would make me cheat?' He was exasperated now, his voice full of frustration.

'I don't know. Maybe.' She looked away, ashamed of her behaviour, except for the fact that she'd lost count of how many nights she'd spent lying in bed wondering if he was with Mary, if they'd grown closer while she'd been thousands of miles away. If he'd slipped, just once.

'I'm sorry,' she said because she didn't want to ruin their time together, even if it meant never knowing the truth. She simply longed for the days when her pain and fear weren't always so close to the surface.

Andre took a steadying breath, then gave her a long look before cupping his hand around her chin and turning her face towards him. 'If you want to know the truth, then yes, sometimes being with Mary has crossed my mind. This year has been hard without you. And she's there, every day, offering an easier life. But I haven't been with her. She's not who I want and she's not the one I love, and if you don't know that by now, then what are we even doing?'

She searched his face. Deep pools of brown stared back at her, the same eyes that had never lied to her before, and she knew with certainty that he wasn't lying now.

She rolled over onto her stomach and laid her head on his pillow. He slid down again and placed his head beside hers, so that they were touching.

'I've missed you,' she said. 'And I know I'm asking awful questions and I sound insecure, but this isn't a normal situation.'

'I know it's not. It's hard for me too.'

'Maybe after two years I can apply for an Italian visa and come back to Rome.'

'Can we do this for two more years?'

His question made her breath seize, but he was right to ask it. How could their relationship endure such distance, constantly testing them? How long could she despair over Mary and all the things she couldn't control?

Two years was a long time.

FOURTEEN

After a shower together, they dressed and went in search of food. Daylight faded and the wind had picked up, gusting under a navy sky. They found a restaurant near the hotel and ordered dinner and wine, followed by several espressos.

It was good to do normal things, to be in each other's presence without the hindrance of time zones and video calls. Belle could hold Andre's hand, lean in to kiss him whenever she liked and sip espressos with the explicit intent that they would be awake all night. And there was no mention of Callum, for which Belle was grateful. For the past four days, he'd been all she could think about—who was he, where was he, how would he receive the news that she was his? Her head ached with the constant questions.

And had it only been four days? She felt like she'd been in Scotland for weeks, chasing Callum's shadow, following a trail of crumbs that promised so much, only to peter out within sight of her goal. So consuming was her quest to find him that it was a relief to let him go for a while and focus her energy on the beautiful man in front of her. As she drank her third espresso, her ankles entwined around

Andre's under the table, she thought of Riley, hoping she'd found comfort too, in the arms of her bartender. Paris had thrown them so far off course that she sometimes wondered if either of them would ever make it back.

Well after midnight, with the caffeine having done its intended work, they walked down to the beach and slipped off their shoes, feeling the cold sand between their toes, before taking the winding path through Castle Green back to the hotel. Once inside, it took Andre seconds to remove her clothes and have her back under the covers, as the black night inched towards a half-hearted dawn then eventually, a frosty sunrise. All time was lost in a blur of white sheets and entwined limbs. If there was ever a time to breathe Andre in, to saturate her soul with his, it was now, for their days were numbered again.

Being with him, lying close to him, threw her back to a time in Italy when they'd enjoyed slow walks through the piazza and sat side by side at the staff dinners, the air charged with their attraction, the same powerful chemistry that had sustained them so far. It allowed Belle to cling to the hope that maybe they *could* do this. That stolen moments and chance encounters might be enough to see them through if they both held on.

The next morning, after only a few hours of sleep, they rose. Coffee was the order of the day, and they drank several cups over bacon and pancakes at a café nearby. Belle's thighs were pleasantly tender, her body aching in places that still bore the memory of Andre's hands. She was certain nothing could deflate the bubble she'd cocooned herself in until he brought up the subject of Fort William.

'Have you thought about going?' he asked.

'I have, just not in the last twenty-four hours. I've been

thinking about other things.' She reached for his hand and brought it to her lips, kissing it playfully.

His expression told her he wasn't fooled. 'Belle, I'm serious.'

'So am I,' she said. 'Can I not block out the world and enjoy you for a bit?'

He smiled. 'Of course you can, but I have to leave in a couple of days. If you want to go to Fort William, then I want to come with you. I have the rental car. I can drive us there.'

Belle squirmed in her chair. She let his hand drop and picked up her coffee instead, taking a sip. Andre's eyes followed her. 'I'm not sure.'

'About which part?'

'About going to Fort William. What if Callum doesn't want to know about me?'

'I don't think that will happen.'

'Carlota said he left her because she asked to start a family with him.'

Andre sat back and sighed. 'Is that what this is about? You think he never wanted children so why would he want you?'

'I've spent my whole life not being good enough for Edward,' she said. 'And I wasn't good enough for Ben. I can't be a disappointment to Callum as well.' What would that say about her? That she was a complete failure? That something was wholly and fundamentally wrong with her? She'd always struggled with confidence and the thought that Callum might see the same flaws in her as her father and Ben had swallowed her as thoroughly as a riptide.

'Callum doesn't know you enough to make that assessment,' Andre said. 'And if he turns you away, at least you'll know where you stand. You'll never be left wondering.'

While he spoke reason, she took only mild comfort in it. She may have arrived on Scotland's shores with a reckless, wayward hope, but the fear of being turned away by Callum had always bubbled near the surface. Now dread and consternation had become impervious, and it over-whelmed her.

Andre's eyes crinkled with concern as she suspected her internalisations had played out on her face. 'Look, whatever happens in Fort William, I'll be right beside you. We'll do this together. And if your real father doesn't want to get to know you, then it will be his loss. You can go home knowing that you tried. And the regret will be his, for how could anyone *not* love you?'

She leaned across the table and pressed her lips to his, as his fingers slipped through her hair, wrapping around the back of her neck, pulling her closer. Sometimes it scared Belle how much she loved Andre, how she could anchor herself completely to him if she allowed it. It was as though he'd been created just for her, that's how perfectly they fit together. He saw the good in her that the men before him hadn't always seen.

Did she swallow her fears and go to Fort William, or did she return home, never knowing what could have been? The latter would save her heart, of course, but the wonder-ing, the regret, would follow her around forever, and she carried enough regret on her shoulders to last a lifetime.

She sat back in her chair and nodded reluctantly. 'Okay, let's go to Fort William.'

BELLE TEXTED Riley with the plan then, the next morning, she and Andre packed their bags and left

Broughty Ferry for Fort William. The day was overcast and cold as they inched their way back across Scotland, following a trail of towering hillsides and deep valleys dusted with meadow saffron. Blue-green mountains grazed the clouds and distant cottages clustered around pearly lochs, their surfaces glassy beneath the sky.

The drive was not quite three hours. They stopped at a small town for coffee and breakfast, the café perched by the pier of an enormous inlet. It was colder there than it had been in Broughty Ferry, the wind whipping through Belle's coat and scarf, as Andre shivered too.

'Slightly cooler than Rome's autumn,' he said, blowing warm air onto his hands as they left the café and crunched back through newly fallen leaves, their breath cloudy on exhale.

They arrived in Fort William at midday, accompanied by a light shower and a brisk breeze. The town basked in the shadow of great Ben Nevis, Loch Linnhe below reflecting the deeply ridged peaks on the mountain's surface. The town was charming, but the broody architecture and leaden sky made everything seem dark.

The high street was mostly pedestrianised, so Andre found a parking spot several blocks away and parked the car. Unlike Balloch or Broughty Ferry where they'd had a work-place or residential address to begin with, in Fort William they were clueless. On the drive over, feeling panicked, Belle had texted Mrs Murray to ask her if Hamish had heard from Callum yet. Twenty minutes later, she replied with a disheartening, *No sorry, lass. I've been asking him, but he hasn't.*

'We could start on the high street and search all the restaurants and pubs asking if anyone knows him,' Andre suggested, turning the car off. 'The town isn't that big; we can work our way outwards. If he's here someone will know him.'

He looked entirely invested in her mission and she loved him even more for being there by her side. She glanced out the window watching the rain pursue them in earnest. It wasn't the greatest weather to be searching for a needle in a haystack. 'I'll call Riley and find out where she is.'

It turned out that Riley was close, her car already parked not far from where they were. Through rivers of rain trickling down the windscreen, Belle saw her dashing up the street towards them. She opened the backdoor and dived in, her hair stuck to her face and her clothes soaked through.

'Anytime Callum wants to wave his hand and tell us where he is, that would be great,' she muttered, wringing her hair out. 'This weather is the pits.'

'How was Balloch?' Belle asked, turning in her seat to face her.

Riley smiled. 'Most satisfying.'

'Is the drought over?'

'And then some.'

Andre grimaced. 'Leo will be devastated.'

'Leo should marry an Italian girl,' Riley said, 'and make his mama happy.'

'He wants to marry you.'

Riley rolled her eyes. 'I haven't got a century to wait for that to happen.'

'What's the plan?' Belle asked, eager to steer them back on track.

'We'll probably need to do this the hard way and go from place to place, see if anyone's heard of him,' Andre said. 'I think it's the only option unless Carlota gave you more information about where he is.'

Belle shook her head. 'All she knew was that he'd headed west to here. I don't think she knows any more than that.'

Andre nodded. 'Then we do this the old-fashioned way. Cold asking.'

Riley glanced out the window at the soggy street. 'We're not allowed to drive down the high street. It's for foot traffic only. We're going to have to walk.'

'I'll make a list of all the restaurants, hotels and pubs in Fort William and mark them off as we go,' Andre suggested. He pulled his phone out and googled places to visit. There were sixty-two establishments across Fort William and Lochaber where he thought they should ask, and Belle was relieved once again that he was there. Her emotions were running too high, her thoughts too scrambled to be able to think logically and plan.

During a brief respite in the weather when the rain eased to a shower, they climbed out of the car and darted under a narrow awning, water leaking over the sides and dripping onto their heads. Once they'd gathered themselves—Riley grumbling about their absurdity scouring Scotland without an umbrella—they hurried towards the high street. When they arrived, they quickly walked into the first pub they saw. Stale lager and warmth greeted them as they stepped inside. A bartender passed them, carrying a tower of glasses, and Andre immediately flagged him down.

'Excuse me, can you help us?'

The middle-aged man with greying hair and a beard paused. 'Sorry, this bar is closed, but the one out the back is open.'

'Actually, we're looking for a friend who we think lives in the area,' he said. 'Callum MacKenzie.'

The man's bushy eyebrows drew together. 'Callum MacKenzie?'

'He's a chef, and likely to be working in a pub or restaurant. Probably within the last four months,' Belle added.

'So he's fairly new to the area?' the bartender asked, precariously balancing the glasses. 'I'm sorry. I dinnae know anyone by that name. He doesnae work here. Ye could try a few of the other pubs along High Street or around Glen Nevis.'

'Thank you,' she said. She was disappointed but hardly surprised. It would have been lottery-winning luck to have found him in the first place they tried.

They left the pub and perched under its awning, out of the rain.

'Damn, it's cold,' Riley said, her breath foggy.

'Let's try a few more places, then we can find a hotel,' Andre suggested.

They crawled along High Street, moving from bar to restaurant to café, asking the same questions, trying to flush Callum out. They tried their luck at several bed and breakfasts too, but no one had heard of him.

'If he's here, he's not well-known,' Belle said, disheartened. Maybe Carlota had been wrong about Fort William, perhaps intentionally so. She'd mistaken Belle and Riley as her replacement in Callum's life. There was every chance she'd sent them in the wrong direction on purpose.

Andre glanced again at his phone. 'We still have plenty of places left on the list. He might not be in this part of town.'

They walked back to the car as the rain poured down, turning the streets into a torrent.

'Let's find somewhere to stay,' Belle said. 'It's going to be dark soon and this weather isn't letting up.' And as much as she wanted to find Callum, the helplessness had returned, the kind that came when you chased a shadow, only to find you could never quite wrap your hands around it. Their mission was producing fewer leads and more dead ends, and while Callum had to be *somewhere*, every turn of the corner grew colder. Sleep, food, a hot shower, and a press of the reset button would hopefully restore perspective. The fact that Andre would leave Scotland soon was just another thing she didn't want to contemplate.

FIFTEEN

They had a quiet dinner at the hotel restaurant, situated on the high street. The waitress serving them, Cathy, had a mane of flowing red hair and was exuberant and chatty. Andre was quick to ask her if she knew Callum.

Her eyes went upwards as she thought. 'Callum MacKenzie. Callum MacKenzie,' she repeated to herself. 'Now that ye mention it, the name does sound familiar, but I can't say why.'

'Is he in hospitality—a chef maybe?' Belle asked, hope rising in her chest the way it often did when she was thrown a crumb.

Cathy shrugged. 'I really dinnae know, only that I've heard the name before. I've never met the man, but Fort William and Lochaber aren't big places. I'm sure if ye search hard enough and ask enough people, yer bound to stumble across him.'

Cathy served them plates of neeps and tatties swimming in thick, hot gravy, with drams of whisky that glowed bronze near the fireplace. They ate in the comfortable fug of the dining room and Cathy's unfailing Scottish cheerfulness made Belle finally relax. Her head stopped spinning with thoughts of Callum, and it was nice to have that brief respite as she talked and joked about less serious things.

Andre regaled them with stories of new waiters dropping plates of food and how his father seemed to terrify every new sous chef who started. He told them about the summer that had just passed, the cold winter that was coming, and how he sometimes still walked past Avery's flat and sat down on the front steps.

Belle's throat tightened at the mention of it. That flat had been the cornerstone of her time in Rome—the place where her relationship with Andre had blossomed. Where she'd fallen in love with him, talking on those steps for hours until dawn. It was the place where Avery was and always would be, in her memories.

After another glass of whisky, Riley retired to her room, protesting days of lack of sleep, and Belle and Andre followed shortly after to theirs, Andre running a bath for them.

Belle slipped out of her jeans and jumper, her skin sticky from wet clothes that had stuck to her, then dried. She scooped up her long hair, tied it in a loose bun, then slid into the hot water, watching Andre undress and slide in opposite her. Water almost sloshed over the sides, and he grinned like a little boy who had come close to making a mess.

She pushed off the edge, turned and came to rest between his legs, with her back to his chest. His arms went around her, his lips on her neck as she rested her head against him.

'It's been a long day, no?' he murmured.

'A long day. A long month. A long year.' Everything felt

weighted, her muscles, her heart, her motivation to keep going. Her brain was soggy and exhausted.

'We will find him,' Andre said, sensing her thoughts.

'I'm not sure anymore,' she said. 'Maybe it's better if I don't, for Mum's sake and for Dad's.'

There was a soft rumble in his throat. 'There is nothing wrong with wanting to know who your father is. After all these years, you deserve that. You are not betraying anyone by looking for him.'

He always knew what to say, and from her spot between his legs, she swivelled around in the water to face him. She cupped her hands around his cheeks and brought his lips to hers. 'What would I do without you? Just when I feel myself losing faith, you put everything into perspective.'

He grinned. 'I just wish you listened more.'

She chuckled, touching her forehead to his, steam rising from their skin. 'You are everything to me,' she said.

'And you are the best part of me.'

'I don't want to be separated anymore.'

'We'll be together again soon.'

'When?' she asked. Searching his face, she could see he didn't have the answer to that question. The day after tomorrow he would leave, and their relationship would be put to the test once more. Then there was Mary, the mere thought of the woman doubling her fears in an instant.

She trusted Andre, but out of sight could also become out of mind. After Ben, and the older she became, she found herself less inclined to trust unreservedly. Trust was fickle— you could pour it all into one person but if they didn't care for it, didn't wrap it tight and hold it close and nurture it with respect, it could disintegrate.

Andre was watching her closely, dark eyes flickering

across her face. 'I can see your brain working. I know the things you worry about. Mary... me.'

'I can't help it,' she whispered.

'I think of those things too,' he said. 'I constantly worry about who will come into your life while I'm not there. Who will hold you when I can't.'

'There hasn't been anyone else.'

'Yes, but for how long? I know your chef friend likes you—what's his name? Kieran. I saw it the last time I visited, the way he looked at you.'

'Nothing's happened,' she said, feeling the sting of his insinuation, knowing how he must have felt when she'd accused him of the same.

'And I believe you. But we're both lonely.' He sighed deeply, sadly. 'I just miss you. Every second of every day I'm wondering about you, and it drives me crazy. I wake in my bed without you, and it hurts, like physical pain.' He pulled her closer to him so that her chest was against his, their skin pressed together. His eyes were warm, like the burnished browns of a forest at sunset. She would never know eyes like his again.

Belle let his words wrap around her. Their relationship was what it was—strong, unyielding, yet so fragile it could shatter like glass.

She placed her lips on his, parting his mouth with her tongue, her hands moving across his chest, down to his hips.

'I love you,' he panted huskily, his hand reaching to the back of her neck. 'I'll never love anyone like this again.'

'Promise me.'

'I promise you.'

Their kisses grew intense. He tasted sensual, like heady summer nights, and she savoured every mouthful of him, bottling the memory of him away for the lonely days ahead when she'd need it most. She bit down on his lip and heard him moan softly, as his hands found her breasts, tracing a path down to her stomach, then settling on her hips where, in one swift motion, he lifted her on top of him, sliding into her.

Her head dropped back as water rushed over the edges of the bath, soaking the floor, their skin hot with steam and her hair damp, his kisses like fire on her body. Every touch, every kiss was a clash of wills, of unconscionable agonies. The press of his mouth, so present, so real, so interminable, would all be a distant dream once he left Scotland. Parting again could well spell the end for them, and the thought reverberated through her like tremors. *We're both lonely.* His words, meant to calm her, only filled her with doubt.

So she held him closer, pushed him deeper, and revelled in the grip of his hands, cursing Fate for the games it played.

———

BY MORNING the rain had moved on and a watery sun rose over Fort William, making the mist curl and cling. Creamy clouds drifted in a pale autumn sky and a light wind pushed stark trees around.

Belle watched from the window, the curtain parted slightly, as the town stirred to life below. Andre was still asleep, but she'd woken early, fretful yet hopeful for the day ahead, faced again with the prospect of meeting her real father as anxiety galloped through her like wild horses.

There was a rustling behind her and she let the curtain fall, walking back to the bed. Andre was stretching, sheets tangled around his body, a body she had enjoyed thoroughly the night before. She climbed onto the bed and snuggled up to him, his arms drifting lazily around her to pull her in.

'Good morning,' he said, his voice thick with sleep. His fingers traced her shoulder, and she placed a hand on his chest.

'Morning.'

'Ready to find Callum today?'

'I am,' she said. 'Where should we start?'

'Let's finish searching Fort William before lunch, then we can move further out. I have every intention of finding him before I fly home tomorrow. I don't want to miss your reunion.'

'Don't talk about leaving,' she said. 'It makes me too sad.'

'And yet, it's all we can think about.'

She drew herself up to him and kissed him full on the mouth. 'Then we should make good use of our time left. It can't be all tavern-hopping.'

He grinned, rolling on top of her and pinning her beneath him. 'I was thinking the same thing.'

They were late getting down to breakfast. Riley was already on her second cup of coffee, the remnants of cereal and toast before her. Belle and Andre ate, downed a quick espresso, then the three of them hurried out the door, keen to start the search before the weather turned again.

As they walked, Andre produced his phone and retrieved a list of places he'd compiled for the day's search. 'We have a few more to visit in the town here, then we can drive over to Ben Nevis and Glen Nevis and try these places.' He pointed further down the list.

'What if he's on the fringe of Fort William and we miss him altogether?' Belle asked.

'It's possible,' Andre said, scrubbing his hand over his jaw. 'But hopefully, someone will have heard of him and can point us in the right direction. It only takes one person to know.'

'Like Cathy,' Riley said. 'She thought the name sounded familiar.'

They returned to where they'd left off the day before, visiting the places on Andre's list and asking if Callum worked there or if anyone knew him. They were met with the same answer each time.

No. Sorry.

Ne'er heard o' th' guy.

Maybe try next door.

There had been several close calls, causing Belle's heart to canter. *We have a Callum, but he's nae a MacKenzie.* Or *we have a MacKenzie, but he's nae a Callum.* Then her hopes would flag again, and they would trudge on to the next place.

By the time they'd finished most of the streets in Fort William town, it was lunchtime. They paused for a quick bite and several espressos at a café, then collected the car from the hotel and headed to Ben Nevis. The mountain came into view as they drove, like an ancient giant of the land and not for the first time since she'd landed in Scotland, Belle's breath caught at the beauty of it.

Ben Nevis was exquisite with its mist-shrouded peak—the highest summit in the British Isles, Cathy had proudly informed them the evening before. Glen Nevis below was equally as enchanting, wrapping itself around the mountain's southern flank, its valleys and grooves filled with low clouds.

From inn to restaurant they drove, asking if anyone knew Callum. The question was growing weary on Belle's lips, sounding flatter every time she asked it, and feeling even flatter when the same resounding no was received.

Late in the afternoon, they swung into the small carpark of a restaurant that was a restored nineteenth-century church. The air was growing chillier as the sun dropped and the shadow of the mountain cooled the town.

Inside the restaurant, in a front room lined with dark oak panelling and a snapping fireplace, Andre led them to a bar where a bartender was pouring a beer for a patron. After the patron left, the bartender smiled and greeted them.

'What kin I get ye?' he asked. He had cheery blue eyes and was clean-shaven, a crop of blond hair falling over his face as he gave Riley an appreciative glance.

'We're looking for a friend of ours,' Andre said. 'He lives and works in the area.'

'Och, who might that be?'

'Callum MacKenzie,' Belle supplied. 'He told us where he worked, but we forgot the name of it. We thought it might be here.'

It was a well-rehearsed line, for most people had begun to regard them warily when asked for information. They found the more nonchalant they appeared, the more likely people were to assist them.

'Callum?' the bartender said immediately, throwing Riley an eager grin, only too happy to help in the presence of a beautiful woman. 'Aye, he's here. Works in the kitchen.'

Belle gripped the bar, her legs almost buckling. 'Callum? He's here?'

The bartender raised an eyebrow. 'Aye. Callum MacKenzie. That's who you're looking fur, right?'

'Yes... yes, we are.' She tried not to appear too shocked in case the bartender grew wary of them too. Andre's hand was on her back, and she turned and found his steady gaze, his eyes telling her to breathe.

'Any chance you could bring him out?' Riley asked sweetly.

The guy nodded, compliant. 'Yeah. Sure. Easy! Just wait here a minute.' He stepped out from behind the bar and left the area, disappearing through a doorway.

They all let out a collective breath. It was hardly the work of a moment, countless days and hours spent following Callum's trail, from coastline to coastline, but somehow, through perseverance and sheer luck, they'd found him, and Belle's pulse began to roar in her ears.

The minutes were interminable as she waited for him to arrive, her foot relentlessly tapping the timber floor, only half-listening to Andre and Riley talking. Soon her father would stride back through that doorway, and she would recognise him—his eyes, his smile, the way he spoke—and she hoped he would recognise her, in the same way that Hamish had. Her heart drummed hard against her ribcage, and she worried it would burst out of her chest.

Andre reached for her hand and held it firmly in his own. 'You're okay,' he whispered.

Riley too had a wide-eyed, expectant look on her face.

Footsteps sounded along the floor, and the bartender and another man stepped through the doorway back into the front room.

'This is Callum,' the bartender announced, leading him to them.

Belle stopped breathing. The man was only marginally taller than her petite size, with enormous brown eyes and a jovial disposition. His stomach was round beneath his sauce-splattered apron, and he had a thick grey beard that framed a kind but confused smile.

'Hello,' he said. 'How kin I help ye?'

Belle fought to find her words, words she had rehearsed for this moment but that had suddenly deserted her.

He was looking at them all, expectant, and Andre cleared his throat. 'Belle?'

'Yes, um...' She swallowed hard. 'I've been looking for you.'

Callum's brow creased. 'Ye have?'

'Yes, uh... because... I think you knew my mother when she came here about thirty-eight years ago.' Her face was on fire, her armpits clammy. Everyone was staring at her.

Callum stuck his hands on his hips. 'I see. Who would that be?'

'Grace.' She watched his face for a sign of recognition, but disappointingly saw none. 'You met her in Kirkcudbright and travelled together around Scotland. When she arrived back home, she realised she was pregnant. And so...' She took a gulp of air, 'and so I believe you're my father.' Oh God, there it was. Out of her mouth. And yet, as she still searched his face, he looked even more confused.

To her astonishment, he threw his head back and roared with laughter.

Riley glanced at her and shrugged. Andre shot him a look of disapproval.

When Callum got a hold of himself, he crossed his arms and stood with his stocky legs apart. 'I'm sorry,' he said, his shoulders still quaking with amusement. 'I dinnae mean to laugh.'

'Then why are you?' Andre asked.

Callum's chest trembled with quiet chuckles. 'Because that's impossible.'

'Impossible?' Belle asked.

'Aye. Fur one, I've never been to Kircudbright before. And two...' he held up his left ring finger, 'I'm happily married to my husband. In fact, I've never been with a woman in all my life. I hate to disappoint ye, but I couldn't possibly be your father.'

Belle shrank with humiliation, her hands flying to her mouth, wanting to stuff her declaration back inside it. 'Oh, God, I'm so sorry!' Her face flushed a bright shade of beetroot.

He laughed again and patted her shoulder. 'Dinnae be sorry fur me. I'm sorry fur you. You're a bonnie lassie, and you've clearly travelled a long way to find him. Believe me, I'd love to be yer da, but I'm just nae the guy you're looking fur.'

'Do you know any other Callum MacKenzies in the area?' Riley asked.

Belle was glad someone's brain still worked because she was too mortified to speak.

'Sorry, no, but it's nae an uncommon name in Scotland.' Callum smiled encouragingly at Belle. 'Have ye tried social media? Or one of those ancestry sites?'

'I have,' she murmured, too embarrassed to look him in the eye. 'But I might need to try again.'

Callum nodded warmly, sincerely. He looked genuinely sorry for her. 'Well, I wish ye luck, lassie. Ye have a fighting spirit, I'll give ye that. Yer da is one lucky man to have a daughter like you looking fur him.'

SIXTEEN

They left Glen Nevis and returned to Fort William under darkening skies. Andre parked the car in the hotel carpark just as the heavens opened and rain gushed down. They headed immediately to the bar and found Cathy there, the dining room waitress who doubled as a barmaid in the afternoons. They slid into stools at the bar and as she poured them tumblers of whisky, Belle told her of their encounter with Callum MacKenzie that afternoon. She admitted that she'd thought he might be her biological father, but how he'd confirmed that wasn't possible.

Cathy tried to keep a straight face during the story, but in the end, gave a rasping bark of laughter. 'I'm sorry, I don't mean to laugh. I shouldn't find it funny. This is nae a funny situation!' But her shoulders still quaked with her chuckles until Belle gave up feeling so miserable about it all and laughed too. Better than crying, she figured.

'I feel to blame,' Cathy said, finally looking abashed. 'I was the one who told ye about him. I sent ye on yer way with false hope.'

'It's not your fault,' Belle said, cupping her hands

around her glass. 'Nor anybody's. There are hundreds of Callum MacKenzies in Scotland. We were bound to run into the wrong one eventually.'

'Aye, right ye are. It's a common name,' Cathy agreed. 'But I still feel like a numpty. Let me get ye another drink.'

The alcohol ended any further attempt at driving around Fort William. With the weather worsening outside, they remained at the bar. It was warm and dry and the fire was roaring. Cathy plied them with snacks and whisky, some on the house in an apparent peace offering over the Callum mix up. No matter how many times Belle told her she wasn't to blame, she still looked sheepish. But finding the right Callum in a sea of Callums was always going to be a challenge. Belle had been under no illusions about that. And Scotland *did* have a sea of them.

When afternoon bled into evening and the rain stopped, they left the hotel and walked a block to an Italian restaurant Belle had noticed earlier that day. They ordered plates of steaming *ribollita*, swordfish with capers, pan-fried gnocchi with hazelnuts and sage, and bottles of Barolo in a trattoria just like the ones in Rome, where music and conversation and garlic were rich in the air. It was the kind of meal Belle had been missing, like the staff dinners at Valentina's, when wine flowed, dishes of food adorned the table and everyone broke bread together. Nowadays her nights were spent in the kitchen at The Olive Grove in Camden, with barely time to eat and no staff dinner to look forward to afterwards.

She missed everything about Rome—the ornate cobbled streets and colourful marketplaces, the street-side bars and haunting ruins. But most of all she missed Andre, even now as he sat across the table watching her intently, for he must have felt it too—how little time they had left. Hours, really, before he was back on a plane to Rome in the morning. Their time together was always bittersweet—a drop in the ocean, days that they could never squeeze enough from before they were over.

Back at the hotel, Riley bid them goodnight and stumbled along the corridor to her room, the wine and whisky making her zigzag and giggle.

Inside their room, Andre pulled Belle to him and pressed his lips to hers. He tasted of wine and butter and a hint of citrus, and he smelled good, so good that she linked her arms around his waist as they both swayed from too much Barolo at dinner. They stood there for a long time, savouring each other.

'Don't go,' she said to him, urgency in her voice.

He rested his forehead against hers and closed his eyes. 'I would stay if I could.'

'Then stay.'

'I can't.'

'Just one more day. Or two. Or forever. Come home with me.'

He didn't answer, sighing deeply instead. What could he say? What made any of it easier? Instead, he unbuttoned her coat and slipped it off her shoulders, his hands working their way under her cable knit to her bare skin.

'Is this all we have left?' she asked.

'No.' But his answer was filled with uncertainty, as though he also struggled to comprehend how they would move forward after Scotland.

She shivered, pulling him closer to her, kissing him with the kind of need her words couldn't always convey. If she couldn't beg him to stay, she would kiss him instead, would commune in caresses until he understood. He responded with gratifying intensity, kissing her back as though the whole world were ending outside their window.

In one liquid motion, Andre removed her jumper and unclipped her bra. He collected her in his arms, wrapped her legs around his hips and carried her to the bed, laying her down, one hand still gripping her waist and the other removing his shirt. They shuffled out of jeans and underwear. Then he was inside her and they were rising and falling against each other like the tide and moon.

Maybe the world *was* ending outside their window. The following day held no promises, just uncertainty—a future together that could be as beautiful as it was unpredictable. And as they passionately and impatiently made love, the time for words was over. There was nothing left to say, nothing that would heal, sustain or satisfy them.

All that was left was that moment, pure and wonderous, intertwined and indistinguishable, achingly bittersweet, and always too fleeting.

———

THE NEXT MORNING, Belle didn't want to stir, didn't want the sun to come streaming through the window, didn't want Andre to sigh and say he'd better get up and pack. They were words that left her feeling cold every time.

Riley knocked on the door to say goodbye to him and they embraced affectionately, like siblings, before she trudged back to her room to sleep off her hangover.

After she left, he took Belle's hand and they went downstairs together with his luggage. Outside at his rental car, he loaded his duffel bag into the backseat and turned to Belle.

'Here we are again,' he said. 'Another goodbye.'

She tried to hold it together. A small part of her had

been revived, sparked back to life by the past few days. Another part of her retreated to a place of desperately missing him and needing to protect her heart. 'We have to find a better way of doing this,' she said. 'We have more goodbyes than any relationship should have.'

He nodded soberly and she couldn't ignore the sinking feeling that overshadowed the good days they'd just had. Where did they go from here? What was next? How long before they saw each other again? And more painfully, who would throw in the towel first? Decide it was all too much. That other, more convenient choices, like Mary, were available.

'Don't look so sad,' he said, tracing his finger down her cheek. 'You break me when you look like that.'

'I don't want you to go.'

'I don't want to go.' He held her close, stroking her hair, dropping soft, desperate kisses onto her head. 'We will see each other again soon.'

'When?' She pulled away to glance at him, but his eyes told her that he was bereft of the answer too.

'I need you to concentrate now,' he said, 'to pour all your energy into finding Callum. He's here somewhere, and you can't go home without knowing who he is.'

She nodded reluctantly, half-hearted and heartsick. 'I will.'

'And call me, every day. I want to know what's happening.'

'Of course. Twice a day.'

He smiled that unassuming smile that hollowed his dimples, melting her every time. 'I should go or I will miss my plane.'

He touched his lips to hers again, deepening the kiss, the last of their minutes together inevitable torture. He would leave and she would remain in that land of keen autumn leaves and blue-green hills, uncertain of the way forward. She wrapped her arms around his neck, holding onto him, savouring the feel of his skin until the next time she saw him, whenever that would be.

He eventually pulled away, glancing regretfully at his watch.

She steeled herself. 'Yes, you'd better go.'

He kissed her one last time, then climbed into the car. She waved at his back window as he drove down the street and around a corner, out of sight.

Belle stood on the street for a long time, the sun struggling through a cold rise, her spirits sapped, watching the place where his car had turned the corner and knowing that it could be the last time she ever saw him. Nothing in life was guaranteed, something she was all too aware of. All illusions eventually melted.

One drop fell, then two, and the sky grumbled and heaved before splitting open. She dragged herself out of the rain and back inside, weighted by all the things she couldn't fix. She longed to lie down again, to draw Andre's pillow close to her, to drift into a sweet sleep for a few more hours so she wouldn't have to think.

But there was still the problem of Callum and where to go from here. The lead Carlotta had given them had turned cold, and they were sitting in Fort William without a next step. Her worst fear was realised; they hadn't a single clue how to find him.

She reached her room, but instead of crawling back into bed, she pulled her phone out of her back pocket and dialled her mother's number. It was early evening in Sydney and after Belle feared her call would go to voicemail, Grace answered.

'Sweetheart,' she said breathlessly. 'How are you?'

'I'm okay. It sounds like I've interrupted you.'

'I was just out in the garden. I wanted to get the cucumber seedlings in the ground before the sun disappeared. Just a sec.'

Belle smiled. Her mother sounded busy and that was good. Planting cucumbers was good. Better than moping around Edward's office, riddled with indecision and guilt over whether to pack it away.

There was shuffling in the background, and Belle knew she was removing her gloves and running her hands through her shoulder-length, stylish hair. She smiled, a gentle longing for home stirring in her chest.

'I'm back.' Grace sounded relaxed. 'Tell me, what's been happening?'

'Andre just left,' Belle said. 'He was with us for a few days.'

'He was? That makes me happy. I need to hear happy things. Is he well?'

Belle smiled. 'Yes. I just miss him already.' She fought a traitorous lump in her throat and sat on the edge of the bed, smoothing her hand over the eiderdown. It was still ruffled from their lovemaking, his soap and cologne still clinging to the air from his earlier shower.

'I understand,' her mother said, sadness edging her words. 'Two people who want to be together should not be kept apart like that. I know how it feels.'

'Because of Callum?'

Grace sighed. 'Yes. I think we could have had a happy life together. Oh, I was happy with your father too, don't misunderstand me. And I miss him terribly, but we're entitled to more than one great love in our lifetime, right?'

Belle thought of Ben, then of Andre, and she agreed.

Each love had taught her something new about loyalty, endurance, and commitment, and how resilient the heart could be. 'Yes, we are.'

'How is the search for Callum going?' Grace asked.

'We've hit a dead-end,' Belle explained. 'We visited the Brook Street address in Broughty Ferry and a woman was living there—Carlota—Callum's ex-girlfriend. She told us that he'd ended their relationship and moved to Fort William four months ago. But he's not here. We can't find him.'

'So you're in Fort William now?'

'Yes.'

'Do you think Carlota was sour about the split? Maybe she gave you false information.'

'I've wondered the same,' Belle said. 'They didn't end on good terms. Even so, I think she was genuine.'

'How did you search for him in Fort William?'

'We visited inns and restaurants, basically any establishment with a kitchen. We didn't get through all of them before Andre left. But it wasn't looking promising anyway. Aside from one false alarm, no one had heard of him. And Mum...' She faltered briefly, wondering whether to bring it up. 'Carlota said Callum left her because she wanted children and he didn't.'

There was a beat of silence. 'And you think that means he won't want you?'

Belle shrugged. 'It's occurred to me. Is that why you didn't tell him about the pregnancy? Because you knew he didn't want kids?'

'No,' Grace said emphatically. 'Not at all. We'd never had that conversation. It was a fleeting relationship, then I left Scotland. I was never meant to see him again *and* I was engaged to your father. It was a very confusing time for me.

And that's why I didn't tell him.' The kettle whistled in the background.

'I just don't know where to go from here. We have no leads and I'm not even sure it's the right thing to do anymore.'

'Callum may not have wanted children with Carlota. It doesn't mean he never wanted them at all.'

'That's what Andre and Riley said.'

'And you should believe them. I took away Callum's right to know you once before. Don't make the same mistake. Give him the chance.' A spoon clinked against a teacup; water pouring.

'So you think I should keep going?' Belle asked.

'Yes. You've travelled a long way to give up now.'

'But how? Where? He's everywhere and nowhere.' And she couldn't visit all the towns in Scotland. What if he'd crept over the border into England or slipped further south to Wales? What if he was no longer in the UK and her entire search was in vain?

Or what if he didn't want to be found?

Belle let out a long, exasperated breath. She was chasing a whisper that was growing more silent by the day.

A knock at the door startled her and she heard a muffled, 'Housekeeping.'

'Mum, I have to go. The room's about to be cleaned. I'll call you later.'

'Okay, love, keep me updated.'

They ended the call and Belle walked to the door, opening it.

'Och, I'm sorry,' a young woman said, her hand suspended mid-air as she prepared to knock again. 'I wasn't sure if ye were still in the room. I kin come back.'

'No, it's fine,' Belle replied, stepping aside so the house-keeper could enter. 'Come in.'

The woman moved past Belle and walked immediately to the bed to make it. A tag pinned to her blouse indicated her name was Ella and she wore her long flaxen hair loosely plaited down her back. Keen to keep out of the way, Belle decided to head down to Riley's room, and she moved to the door, clearing her throat to let the woman know she was leaving.

'You're Belle, aren't ye?' the woman asked, pulling the top sheet tight and tucking it in.

Belle paused and turned to face her. 'That's right.'

'You're the one looking fur Callum MacKenzie.' Colour flooded her pale cheeks. 'Excuse my prying, but Cathy is my cousin. She served ye yesterday at the bar. She told me that ye were looking fur him. We weren't blethering or anything. It just came up.'

Thoughts of walking to Riley's were abandoned. Curious, Belle stepped back into the room. 'No, that's okay. And yes, I have been.'

'Well, Cathy mentioned that ye stumbled across a Callum yesterday, but he wasn't the man ye were looking fur. She felt like a right eejit about it.'

Belle smiled. 'She doesn't need to feel like that. It wasn't her fault.'

'Well, there was another Callum MacKenzie that passed through here about four months ago,' Ella said, straightening the quilt. 'He wasn't here long. He caught up with a friend, who happened to be someone I knew, before moving on. We all had a drink together. I was just wondering if he might be yer guy.'

'How old was he?' Belle asked, but the words came out like a whisper.

'Older,' Ella said, glancing sheepishly at her. 'Old enough to be yer da.'

The pocket of air that was caught in Belle's throat released and her heart thudded. *Old enough to be your dad.*

'I hope I haven't spoken inappropriately. I just thought you'd want to know,' Ella said.

'No, that's great,' Belle said, joy bubbling over despite her reservations. 'That's perfect!'

Ella blushed.

'So how long ago was this again?'

'About four months.'

Carlota had said that Callum left Broughty Ferry four months ago. Same name. Older guy. It couldn't be a coincidence. 'And how long was he here for?'

The housemaid fluffed the pillows and placed them neatly on the bed before she straightened. 'He was just passing through. A few days at most. He knew my friend's da and joined us fur a drink one night.'

'And where was he going next?'

Ella's eyes flew up in thought, as though desperate to get it right. 'I'm pretty sure he said Portree.'

'Portree?'

'Isle of Skye. North-west of here.'

'And did he say if he was passing through or working there?'

Ella grimaced through her recollection. 'He said he had a job, but it wasn't in Portree. He was travelling—visiting friends before his start date.'

'So he might not be there anymore?'

'I'm not sure. The friend he was visiting owns a shop. Portree Whisky Emporium or something like that.' She clicked her tongue as though not entirely sure.

'Portree Whisky Emporium,' Belle repeated.

'Or something like that,' Ella reminded her. 'Ye could go there, ask them, and if he's no longer there, follow his trail.'

'Thank you, Ella!' She leapt forward and hugged the girl, who stood rigid in surprise but with a wide grin on her face. 'I can't tell you what this means to me. I'll let you get back to work.' Already deciding she would leave a generous tip at reception for Ella when they left, Belle dashed from her room and down the corridor to Riley's door. She rapped on it several times, detecting shuffling, a bump, then a groan on the other side.

The door swung open, and Riley stood before her, bedraggled and clutching her elbow. 'Oh, it's you. What's wrong?'

'Get dressed and pack your bags,' she said breathlessly. 'We're going to Skye.'

SEVENTEEN

The Isle of Skye was a two-hour drive from Fort William. They checked out of their hotel rooms immediately and began the drive under grey and foreboding clouds. It was a journey to the northwest of Scotland, accompanied by rugged mountains veiled in rolling mist and woodlands that were velvety green from the rain. Bursts of purple Scottish thistle and wild mountain aven swathed limestone verges, the roads smooth, winding and occasionally rutted.

'We spent all that time searching kitchens in Fort William and he wasn't even there to work,' Belle lamented, her hands clenching the wheel. 'We were looking in the wrong place.'

'Carlota should have been more specific with her information,' Riley said resentfully. Her seat was reclined, and large, dark sunglasses covered her bleary eyes.

'To be fair, I don't think she knew what Callum was doing. Someone else told her that he went to Fort William. We were the ones who assumed it was for work.' Belle sighed. 'Thank God for Ella. I don't know what we would have done without her.' Or Cathy and her wagging tongue.

They stopped for coffee and lunch at a small café near Invergarry before arriving at Skye Bridge, which connected the mainland with the Isle of Skye. The weather was still ominous—it had hardly improved since they'd set out from Fort William—and brief spells of showers pelted down, washing out the landscape.

They crossed the bridge over moody Loch Alsh and continued north through Skye to its largest town, Portree. Slick roads curved through mountainous terrain, emerald fields rolled down towards the coast, and low clouds hung over churlish waters. Still, in all her bleak wintriness, Scotland's largest isle of the Inner Hebrides was captivating, its palette of colours beguiling, and Belle felt her heart tug again, like Scotland was calling to her.

Portree was equally enchanting, perched on the east coast in a sheltered, placid bay fringed by high cliffs and towering hills. A rainbow of terraces clustered along the harbour wall—cotton candy pink, pastel blue and sunshine yellow. They were so picturesque that for a moment, Callum wasn't uppermost in Belle's thoughts.

'What's the name of the place again?' Riley asked.

'The Portree Whisky Emporium. Ella said he was visiting someone there. According to Google, it's on this street.' Belle found a parking spot several streets back from the harbour wall by an old church and turned off the ignition.

If Riley was opposed to the idea of trekking through yet another town looking for Callum as hungover as she felt, she was a good sport about it, tugging on her jacket and climbing out of the car.

Belle zipped her coat up against the cold, looping a scarf around her neck and locking the car door. The emporium was a block away and they began walking through the damp wind.

Belle saw the sign for the store first, pointing its red awning out, the words *Portree Whisky Emporium*, just as Ella had quoted, stamped on its front. As they stepped through the door, a bell tinkled overhead and the powerful notes of cereal, oak and malted barley suffused the air. The store was reasonably large and square. Towering wall cabinets were lined with bottles of whisky behind locked glass, and large oak barrels held neat displays of whisky, cheese, crackers, and chocolate.

At the far end, a man stood bent over his bookwork, pen scratching against paper, reading glasses perched low on his nose. He glanced up at the sound of the bell and smiled. 'Good afternoon there. How kin I help ye? Or are ye just having a browse?'

Belle tore her gaze away from the displays and walked to the counter. 'Hi. Actually, we're looking for someone and we're hoping you can help us locate them.'

The man put down his pen and removed his glasses, his smile frozen on his face. 'I kin try. It depends on who it is.'

'Callum MacKenzie,' Belle said. She held her breath the way she always did when she asked someone about him.

'Callum ye say?' the man asked.

'Yes.'

'I do ken of *a* Callum MacKenzie. I'm nae sure if he's the one you're looking fur.'

'Around sixty, from Kirkcudbright and he's a chef,' Belle supplied.

The smile slipped and the man's eyes narrowed cautiously. 'Why are ye looking fur him?'

That question continued to stump Belle, for she'd been steadfast all along that Callum should be the first to know the truth and yet, it was hardly the case anymore. The Murrays, Hamish and Gilroy knew, not to mention Ella and Cathy.

She was about to blurt the truth out when Riley came to the rescue. 'He's a friend of her mother's and he said we could give him a call if we were ever in Scotland. But trying to reach him by phone has been difficult and we remembered that he mentioned your shop, so while we were here, we thought we'd call in.'

Whether he believed them or not was debatable, but he blinked once, then his guarded expression softened. 'I see. Well, Callum *was* here a few months ago visiting. He's gone now though, went on to Inverness to see his sister and her kids. She lives there.'

'His sister? Do you know her name?' Belle asked.

'Lainey.'

'And her surname?' Hope flared in her chest as she held her breath. Knowing who her aunt was could lead her straight to Callum. 'I assume she's married and not a MacKenzie anymore.'

The gentleman nodded, pushing his glasses up his nose. 'Aye, she's married. But I'm nae sure what her new surname is. If I'm nae mistaken, she used to work at one of the hospitals there.' He scratched his head. 'The name of it escapes me now. I'm nae even sure she's still there.'

'Do you have her address by any chance? Or her number?'

'No, sorry, I don't.'

'How about Callum's?' She was trying her luck now. 'Would you be able to give us that? Or an email address. Something. Anything.'

He pursed his lips, then shook his head. 'No, I dinnae

think I should. That wouldn't be right. I kin send him a message and let him ken you're looking fur him.'

Except he's notoriously difficult to get a hold of, Belle thought dispiritedly.

A crack of thunder outside told them the weather was closing in again.

'We should go,' Riley said.

But Belle still had questions. 'We understand he's starting a job soon. Would you happen to know where that is? Since we're a few months behind him, we could skip the towns in between and go straight there.'

The man rubbed his jawline with a thoughtful expression. 'Och, I wish I could recall, lassie, but he said it in passing and I've since forgotten. Edinburgh or Aberdeen, something like that. Callum moves frequently. He loves the challenge of a new kitchen and a new cuisine, and I can hardly keep up.'

Her last thread of hope vanished. 'Never mind. Thanks anyway.'

'Speaking of kitchens,' the man said, holding his index finger up, 'Callum always talks about The Steer Steakhouse in Inverness. He never visits without eating there at least once. Ye could try yer luck. Someone might know him, might know where this new job of his is.'

Belle smiled her appreciation. 'Thank you. We'll do that.'

He glanced at her quizzically. 'Ye know, ye look familiar. Are ye related to him by any chance?'

She tried not to squirm beneath his gaze. 'Sort of.'

'Aye,' the man said slowly, nodding. 'I kin see the resemblance. In fact, ye look just like him. Ye could pass for his daughter if Callum actually had children.' He laughed at his comment. 'Anyway, ye'd better go. There's a nasty storm brewing outside.'

'Thank you again for your help,' Belle called as she and Riley headed for the door, stepping back out into the freezing wind. Dark clouds marched across the sky, rolling over the water. The harbour was grey and groaning, a curtain of rain charging towards them, the air biting at their skin.

They reached the car as the downpour arrived, battering them with wind and hail. Once inside, Belle turned the car on and blasted the heater, water and ice pelting the windscreen like needles.

'I don't want to stay in Portree overnight,' she said, shrugging out of her wet coat and scarf and tossing them onto the backseat.

'You want to drive to Inverness in *this* weather?' Riley glanced out the window with a raised eyebrow.

'The storm will pass.'

'And Inverness will still be there if we wait a little longer.'

'Yes, but *he* won't be.' Without meaning to, her frustration surfaced.

She hadn't thought for a moment that Callum would still be in Portree, and she knew he would no longer be in Inverness either. They were trailing him by three months. Yes, they were finally back on track, but the trail had grown cold once before and it would grow cold again if they didn't move quickly. Time could be unforgiving, information forgotten, just like Callum's friend at the emporium who no longer recalled where his new job was. Edinburgh or Aberdeen—two completely different cities, hours apart.

No, time wasn't on their side. It was constantly against them and yes, Belle *did* want to drive to Inverness in that godawful storm because she didn't want to wait another second for the trail to desert them again.

'Inverness it is then.' Riley sighed, but it was weighted with frustration too.

They were exhausted, hungover, and cold, and Scotland, as beautiful as she was, was taunting them. Inverness was a two-and-a-half-hour drive from Portree, and Belle promised Riley they would find a hotel as soon as they arrived and start their search again in the morning. Riley seemed appeased with the prospect of a bed and settled into her seat as Belle pulled away from the flooded curb, the storm lashing at their windows, turning the world outside opaque.

EIGHTEEN

On the way to Inverness, Andre called Belle to let her know that he'd landed in Rome, and she relayed to him their journey that morning so far. But there was little chance to get into the details. He had to shower and dress for the dinner shift at Valentina's, and she was navigating soggy, winding roads beneath an unrelenting weather system, so they promised to speak later and ended the call.

An hour into the trip, the weather moved past them and the sky finally cleared, the prettiness of the Highlands revealing itself once more. Shimmering lochs wrapped around ghostly valleys and crumbling castles perched on green banks. The sky was mirrored in the water, clouds dragging past, and snow graced distant mountain peaks, white and pristine. She saw her father in all of it—the deep glens, the rising hillsides and the hovering mist. He was everywhere and yet he was nowhere, and she wondered how many towns he would lead her to before she unearthed him. If only Lady Luck would hear her call, or some smiling, benevolent God, at least.

It was almost five in the afternoon when they reached

Inverness. The sun was playing hide and seek with the clouds, lighting up the spires of St Andrew's Cathedral and rippling Loch Ness, so that the water sparkled like pewter.

Exhausted from the past few days, Belle stayed true to her word and they checked into a bed and breakfast near the sullen River Ness, intending to resume the search for Callum in the morning.

They ate dinner in the dining room, then retired early to their room to shower and crawl under the covers. It was hard for Belle to fathom that earlier that morning they'd still been in Fort William, that she'd said goodbye to Andre, then they'd driven all the way to Portree in search of her father. Now they were in Inverness—town number six in her relentless quest.

Sleep was elusive that night as her mind ticked over and she formulated a plan for the morning. She would call the hospitals as soon as she woke and ask for Lainey, hoping that it wasn't too common a first name that there were many of them. Inverness was a large city, and there were likely several hospitals too. Without a surname or knowing what capacity she worked in, it could be difficult to locate her. There was also the possibility that Lainey didn't work at a hospital anymore.

Lainey. Belle's aunt. With kids who were her cousins and an entire extended family beyond that. The thought simultaneously pleased and dismayed her. Not for the first time, she became disheartened at all the lost years and opportunities.

Maybe The Steer Steakhouse would yield better results, a place Callum was said to frequent often. The staff might know him, might be able to offer information. Either way, she lay awake all night, staring at the ceiling, pleading with Inverness to reveal its secrets, for without another lead, there was no place left to go.

———

BELLE WOKE early and was relieved when Riley stretched and yawned soon after. She climbed out of bed and parted the curtains to peer out, relieved to see the sun rising in a mostly clear sky. The River Ness was less churlish-looking than the day before, a pale blue to match the sky, as the current gently pushed into Beauly Firth.

Belle craned her neck for a better look along the riverbank. St Andrew's Cathedral was further up the street, and the parapets and battlements of Inverness Castle could be seen over the church's spires, a place Belle would have loved to have visited if it wasn't for the priority of finding Callum.

While Riley dressed, Belle discovered there were several hospitals in Inverness where Lainey could potentially work. Starting with Raigmore Hospital, she called each of them and spoke with hospital reception. She asked if Lainey worked there and was asked in return what Lainey's surname was, which department she was from and what the medical enquiry was about. Belle couldn't supply any of the details and was promptly informed that strict privacy policies for staff were in place, and they couldn't give out information. After the last hospital on her list was unable to help her, she ended the call and exhaled with exasperation.

'Any luck?' Riley asked from her spot by the mirror, dragging a mascara brush through her lashes.

Belle tossed her phone onto the bed. 'No. It didn't help that I only had her first name. I don't know if she's a doctor, a nurse or a cleaner. And I wasn't calling about a medical matter. They were suspicious of me straight away.'

'The steakhouse opens in two hours,' Riley said, checking her watch. 'We might have better luck there.'

They ordered cappuccinos and toasted sandwiches at a coffee shop next door and waited for the time to pass at a small table inside. Belle tried calling Andre again—their phone call the day before had been so achingly brief—but he didn't answer, and she didn't leave a message, not wanting to disturb him if he was asleep.

The Steer Steakhouse on High Street was easy to find and was open when they arrived. All the way from the coffee shop Belle prayed to the wind and the sky that someone in the steakhouse would know Callum and be able to direct them. To give them an address, a workplace, something more than the phantom they were endlessly chasing.

A woman in her fifties greeted them inside the front door, her grey hair set in a smooth, straight bob. She was purposefully styled, her white blouse and straight black trousers neatly pressed, and a black tie smartly tucked into her black vest. Her name tag read 'Aileen', and she smiled welcomingly at them. 'Hello. Table fur two?'

Belle cleared her throat and stepped forward. 'Not exactly,' she said. 'I was hoping you might be able to help us with something else instead.'

'Och.' Aileen clasped her hands together. 'What kin I do fur ye?'

'We're looking for someone who we think you might know.'

'Okay.' Her carefully stencilled eyebrows rose with intrigue. 'Who might that be?'

'Callum MacKenzie.'

'Callum?' She looked genuinely at a loss. 'I dinnae know that person. Why dae ye believe I would know him?'

'Someone in Portree said we could find him here.'

'Here?' Aileen turned around and glanced behind her into the steakhouse. It was still early and there were only a few patrons seated. 'Wait staff, bar or kitchen?'

'Neither. He's a customer,' Belle said.

Aileen returned her gaze to them, her lips pressed together in contemplativeness. 'I'm sorry. I'm the manager and I dinnae know anyone called Callum who frequents here. Are ye sure it's this place? There are three other steakhouses in the area, although granted we are the biggest and most popular.' She lifted her chin with obvious pride.

'I'm sure it's this one,' Belle said.

'Is there someone else we could ask?' Riley added. 'Maybe a bartender or a chef?'

'That's a good idea,' Aileen said. 'Let me fetch someone fur ye.'

Aileen disappeared into the belly of the steakhouse and Belle exhaled shakily, shooting a glance at Riley. 'This never gets any easier.'

'Which part? The thought of meeting him or losing him again?'

'Both.'

Aileen returned a few minutes later with a short, squat woman wearing chef's whites and a toque. 'This is Fenella,' she announced. 'Our head chef. She knows Callum.'

'*Knew* Callum,' Fenella interjected. 'He used to come in a fair bit.'

Belle's pulse thumped. 'That's great! Do you know where we can find him now?'

Fenella cast a look at Aileen. 'In Kilvean Cemetery.'

Belle blinked. 'Excuse me?'

'Aye. Callum died two months ago.'

'Wait,' Riley said, looking equally as confused. 'Are we talking about the same Callum here?'

'Aye,' Fenella said again, her gaze steady. 'Callum MacKenzie.'

'And he was a chef? From Kirkcudbright?' Belle asked, her voice growing desperate. *No, no, no*. Not her Callum. Not dead.

'Yes, he was quite a good cook as far as I know,' Fenella confirmed. 'I'm nae sure where he was born.'

'Och dear.' Aileen fanned herself. 'Tragic news. I didnae know him myself, but Fenella told me in the kitchen that he was a regular. I'm nae here all the time, ye see, just an occasional day during the week, so I haven't noticed him before.'

'He had family here too. Very sad,' Fenella said.

Seconds passed as Belle absorbed the news. Her worst fear was realised. She was too late. Callum had passed away, the opportunity to meet him lost forever. 'How did it happen?'

'A stroke.'

'Why doesn't anyone else know about this?' she asked. 'Not one person we've spoken to is aware that he died.'

Fenella and Aileen shared an uncertain look.

'His passing was only very recent,' Fenella said. 'I'm nae sure why people dinnae know. I'm sorry. We weren't *that* close.' She crossed her arms defensively.

'Ye look peaky, dear,' Aileen said, regarding Belle warily. 'You're nae going to faint, are ye?'

'No,' Belle said, stepping back. Three sets of eyes assessed her, and she knew she looked as pale and stricken as she felt. 'I'm fine. Thank you. Kilvean, you said?'

'Aye,' Fenella confirmed. 'The cemetery office there can

direct ye to his gravestone.' She looked miffed at being put on the spot, then relieved when Aileen dismissed her back to the kitchen.

'Thank you, Fenella. That will be all.'

His gravestone. The room tilted and Belle dug her shoes into the timber floor to prevent from swaying with it. Adrenalin fled her body, leaving her disheartened and depleted.

'Kilvean Cemetery is only a short drive from here. Nae more than ten minutes.' Aileen was relaying directions to Riley, casting the occasional worried glance at Belle. 'Are ye sure she doesn't want to sit down?'

'She's fine.' Riley took Belle's arm and propelled her towards the door. 'You've been most helpful. Thank you, Aileen.'

Back outside on the street, Belle struggled for air.

'Are you all right?' Riley asked, watching her closely. 'Maybe you *should* sit down.'

'I'm okay.'

'It might not be him.'

Belle threw her hands up in the air with a disbelieving laugh, then began walking up the street towards their hotel. 'One minute he's here, the next minute he's there, now he's dead!'

'It might not be him,' Riley repeated, hurrying to match her stride.

'Or it might be.' Eight days of searching for him, zigzagging all over the country, had led her to the possibility of his death. And while she'd never known him, the reality of losing a father again so soon after the last, was not something she had prepared herself for.

He was quite a good cook. He had family here too. Lainey and her children were in Inverness. What were the odds?

Then Riley's words resounded in her head. *It might not be him.*

They walked in silence back to the hotel, fatigue and melancholy wrapping around Belle, but she focused on placing one foot in front of the other, intent on getting to the car and finding the cemetery.

AILEEN WAS RIGHT. It was a short drive from Inverness' High Street to Kilvean Cemetery, which was sprawled across gently sloping hills. Before leaving their hotel room, Belle completed a search on the cemetery's website and was provided with the location of Callum's grave.

The results led them into the cemetery, past the office and crematorium and around a network of roads curving through plots and trees. Riley was driving and she pulled the car over to the side of the road as torn clouds gusted across a cold sky.

The gravestones were numerous in this part, rows of them covered with flowers and mementoes, marching up the gradient like solemn soldiers. Belle led the way, studying the names on each headstone, some lives taken after many years, some taken too early, small oval photos of the departed staring back at her. And then she found him, an unassuming black marble headstone among many, marked with several recent bouquets of flowers.

She stopped walking and stared down at the headstone, surprised at the emptiness she felt, as though she were mourning a perfect stranger and not her biological father, even though the two were one and the same.

'This is him,' she said to Riley. Her gaze settled on the small picture of Callum, unable to tear herself away from it.

He was not how she'd imagined him to be—balding through the centre of his head, with hazel eyes, a broad smile, and a full face, as though in life he'd been a large man.

Riley began reading the inscription. 'Callum MacKenzie, 1967 to 2022. Fifty-five years old. Oh!'

Belle's gaze left the photo, falling on the inscription too. 'Beloved husband to Maisie. Father to Nessa and Blake. Brother to Bruce and Joan.'

Riley's eyebrows shot up. 'This Callum was *married*. Yours isn't married!'

'Nor does mine have children called Nessa and Blake,' Belle said slowly, rereading the words. 'That we know of.'

'And wouldn't Lainey's name be on this stone too if she were his sister? It only has Bruce and Joan.'

'It's not my dad.' The realisation hit Belle, making her legs wobble with relief. 'It's not my dad!' Her voice echoed off the gravestones and up the hills.

Riley scoffed. 'So Fenella was wrong.'

'Not necessarily. She just didn't have the right Callum. God, my heart's pounding.'

'Bloody Fenella!'

'She wasn't to know. She thought she was being helpful.' Belle let out an unsteady breath, her pulse rising and dipping as though it too, couldn't work out what was going on. It didn't matter that they'd reached another roadblock, she was just glad that Callum, *her* Callum, wasn't in Kilvean Cemetery. That he was still alive somewhere, waiting for her. That their story didn't end there.

'What do we do now?' Riley asked.

'We go back to the drawing board.'

She snorted. 'What drawing board? We haven't got a clue where he is.'

They turned and left Callum's gravestone, as the wind

dusted the cemetery in red and gold leaves and Belle whispered, 'Sorry,' to the man who'd died and the family who mourned him.

As they trekked back to the car, her mind spun with relief but also despair for her circumstance. She was running out of time to find her father. False leads and dead ends had stolen her momentum and she'd made barely any traction. She couldn't stay in Scotland forever and she feared that all she'd done was hurtle along a path to nowhere.

NINETEEN

Belle spent the rest of the afternoon in their hotel room scouring the internet for 'Lainey née MacKenzie'. Even combing through social media failed to produce anything substantial. There were many Laineys, with various surnames, including MacKenzie, all throughout Inverness and Scotland and, like her initial search for Callum on social media, the results were plentiful. She couldn't possibly reach out to the hundreds of Laineys in existence and explain her situation.

'His end destination is where his new job is at. Didn't the guy at the emporium say that?' Riley was sprawled across her bed, hands tucked beneath her head. 'He said Edinburgh or Aberdeen.'

'Two vastly different cities, one of them the capital of Scotland,' Belle said.

'So we pick one, we go, and we search.'

'On foot? Every commercial kitchen in every bar, restaurant, hotel and inn?'

'Yes,' Riley said. 'Just like we did in Fort William.'

'That could be thousands of places. Fort William doesn't even compare to the size of Edinburgh or Aberdeen.'

'I don't see any other alternatives.'

Belle sighed, glancing at the hopeless search on her phone again. This MacKenzie family was becoming harder to unearth than the Loch Ness Monster, and she wondered again if a DNA search on an ancestry site would be far less problematic. 'Fine. We might as well.'

'Pick a city. Edinburgh or Aberdeen.'

'Aberdeen is closer to us, but Edinburgh is bigger, and perhaps a more likely place for him to seek employment.' Not that she had any idea what went on in the mind of a father she didn't know.

Riley clapped her hands together. 'Edinburgh it is.'

THEY WERE UP with the rising sun the next morning, conceding defeat in Inverness and moving on to Edinburgh. Belle was overcome with déjà vu as they travelled back across the country, passing the familiar lochs and mountains of the granite Highlands, and the valleys and estuaries of the Central Belt that they'd passed previously.

Her mind was foggy as she drove, dreams of Ben and Paris pervading her sleep the night before, and she had a persistent tickle in her throat that she couldn't clear. They stopped for breakfast in Aviemore as weak morning light clung to the mist and a pale sun struggled to rise.

'Edinburgh.' Belle sighed tiredly, wrapping her hands around a hot cup of coffee.

'Yes. It's going to be a long shot,' Riley agreed, biting into a fresh buttery laden with globs of butter and jam. 'I just wish we'd thought to ask Carlota for Callum's mobile number. She was angry enough to give it to us too. It could have saved us a whole lot of time.'

'Carlota thought we were his lovers,' Belle said wryly. 'She would never have given us his number.'

'Hamish then.'

'Hamish said he was notoriously hard to get hold of. Would it have mattered if we'd had it?'

'You could have left a message and at some point, Callum would have seen it. The guy can't fall completely off the grid.'

'Maybe,' Belle said. 'But I wouldn't give out your number if a stranger asked. Just like Gilroy refused to. He was protecting his friend.'

'But you're not a stranger to Callum. You're his daughter, and Gilroy and Hamish knew that.'

Belle shrugged, disheartened. 'Maybe they had an inkling as to how he'd react. They're saving me from the heartache. Or maybe he's aware by now that I'm searching for him and he's purposely avoiding me.' It was a thought she'd tried to push from her mind ever since Carlota had mentioned that Callum hadn't wanted children with her. If Riley was right and he hadn't dropped off the grid, then someone must have told him about her. And that could mean only one thing—he was avoiding her.

They reached Edinburgh by late afternoon and checked into a hotel. Nothing about their search in Scotland's capital was going to be easy, and they both agreed it was important to settle into a hotel room quickly. Belle was also resigned to the fact that Edinburgh would likely be the last city where they could search for Callum. The cost of travel and hotels had left a significant dent in her savings, and the two extra weeks Carlo had granted her were almost up. She could no longer ignore reality as it knocked at her door.

Edinburgh beckoned them out in the early evening, and they tumbled into a seafood restaurant on the corner of a street lined with Old Town's dark granite facades. Of course, Belle asked if anyone there knew Callum, and the answer was no. And perhaps, just for one night, Belle could live with that. She wanted to enjoy her meal, have a glass of wine, and not have to think about maps and streets and establishments and asking the same question repeatedly until her ears rang with the words.

They returned to the hotel under a bruised sky and while Riley watched television, Belle showered. Exhaustion had crept into her bones, her muscles aching, and she longed to climb into her pyjamas and under the covers to sleep. The whole ordeal of losing one father and attempting to find another had caught up with her, and she'd barely had the chance to exhale, let alone come to terms with either. She only hoped it was stress that was making her body so utterly weary and not something she was coming down with.

BELLE TOSSED and turned all night. The tickle in her throat had grown rough, and a chill ran through her so that she grappled for comfort.

'You don't look good,' Riley said the next morning, as she stepped out of the bathroom, a towel wrapped around her body and another around her head. 'Nightmares again?'

'No. I couldn't get comfortable.' She coughed and reached for a tissue on the nightstand, blowing her nose. 'I must have caught a cold.'

'Don't give it to me.' Riley took a cautious step back. 'Maybe you should rest today. I'll go out and ask around.'

'No.' Belle pushed the covers off. 'I want to come. Give me a minute and I'll get dressed.'

They ate breakfast at a café next door. Then, armed with their list of places to visit, they trekked through the Old Town and around Edinburgh Castle asking after Callum, before crossing over into the New Town. After lunch, they circled back to the Old Town and by late afternoon, rain brought their futile quest to a halt. They huddled beneath an awning on the Grassmarket hoping it would pass, but it only grew heavier as though it were setting in for the evening.

Belle's lungs erupted and she coughed, her nose dripping like a tap and her throat on fire. She longed to lay her head down somewhere and close her eyes.

'You're burning up,' Riley said, touching Belle's forehead with the back of her hand.

'It's nothing.' Belle shivered, unable to get warm despite her jacket and scarf wrapped tightly around her.

'Come on, let's get you back to the room. Enough for today.'

At the hotel, Riley pulled the covers down, helped Belle change into pyjamas and put her to bed. 'You need to sleep. You're no good to anyone like this.'

'But Callum...'

'No more Callum today. Just rest.'

Riley plonked down on her bed with her phone and Belle closed her eyes, sleep coming so swiftly, she barely registered its arrival.

WHEN SHE WOKE AGAIN it was dark. Shadows on the walls were moonlit, and a siren wailed on the street outside;

the commonplace sounds of a city. Riley was in the next bed, snoring softly, her silhouette gently illuminated.

Belle coughed. Her eyelids were heavy like bricks and her chest was weighted as though someone was sitting on it. She groaned and pulled the covers up to her chin, unable to get warm.

'Are you all right?' asked Riley groggily from across the room.

'Sorry, I didn't mean to wake you,' Belle wheezed. Every part of her hurt.

'You've been tossing and turning all night,' Riley said. 'Should I ring for a doctor?'

'It's just a cold,' Belle said. 'I'll be fine by the morning.'

'Okay.' Riley's voice was laden with sleep. 'Wake me if you need me.'

But Belle wasn't fine by the morning. If anything, she felt worse. Sleep had been fractured by fever and a dry cough that irritated her lungs and grated her throat.

'We have to search for Callum,' she croaked from her bed, as she watched Riley move around the room, tidying up.

'No Callum today. You're sick. You can't possibly walk around the city like that.'

'But we're wasting time. And I can't stay in Scotland forever.' Falling ill was the worst thing that could have happened. Her funds were low, her annual leave was running out, and being held hostage by a virus in her hotel room wasn't helping.

'I'm going to call downstairs for a doctor,' Riley said. 'I'm sure the hotel can supply one.'

'I don't need a doctor,' Belle said, burrowing deeper under the covers. 'There's nothing he or she can do for me.'

'They can give you antibiotics.'

'It's just a virus. I'll have a couple more hours' sleep, then I'll be ready to search.'

She drifted off again, waking briefly to witness the morning become afternoon. When she finally opened her eyes properly, it was to a darkening room, city lights flicking on and music blaring from the bars downstairs.

'Take these.' Riley was by her side, handing her two pills. 'It's paracetamol.'

'How long was I asleep for?' she asked, accepting them, and gulping them down with water.

'The whole day, which is not a bad thing. You clearly needed it.'

'Callum,' she rasped.

'I did a little searching while you slept, but I couldn't find him. I'll try again tomorrow.'

'I'll come with you,' Belle said, falling back onto her pillow. That small effort was enough to expend her energy.

'Just rest and recover. We'll talk about it in the morning.'

Later that night, while Riley slept too, the pills took effect and Belle's fever broke. She walked weakly to the bathroom and showered, scrubbing her stale hair and sour skin. After brushing her teeth and changing into clean pyjamas, she climbed back into bed and fell into a dreamless sleep. But by morning, the fever had returned and so had the wretched sweats.

As Riley rose and dressed, Belle tried to climb out of bed too. 'Wait for me,' she gasped.

Riley shook her head emphatically. 'No way. You're in no condition to be out there walking.'

'But—'

'You need to rest. You're sick. If I find anything, I'll come straight back and tell you.'

Riley left and Belle's rising sense of helplessness wasn't

enough to keep sleep at bay. She slept some more, the light in the room changing every time she opened her eyes. Sometimes Riley was there, sometimes she wasn't, but there was always the constant noise of outside penetrating the windows—sirens and music and laughter—until her head ached with it.

Night bled into morning, and at times she wasn't sure what day it was or how long she'd been bedridden, only that she felt weaker and sicker than she'd ever felt before. She hardly ate—only a nibble of takeout that Riley brought in, usually something fried and extraordinarily greasy—and she attempted to drink water, but the effort of doing anything other than sleeping was arduous. Her neck was stiff, and her body ached with fever.

On day three—or was it four?—she awoke to find Riley walking to and from the bathroom, packing their belongings.

'What are you doing?' she asked, trying to sit up, but the room spun.

'We have to leave. We only booked this room for four nights and they have another guest waiting to come in. There aren't any other rooms available, so we're going to have to check out.'

'Are we flying home?' The idea of boarding a plane as sick as she was made her bones feel heavier and besides, she was still determined to find her father, even with her body shutting down.

'Not yet. But I'm pulling the pin on Callum for now. You're in no fit state to do anything but rest. I'm taking you somewhere quiet where you can get a decent, nourishing meal.'

On the heels of that statement, Belle faded again, the sheer effort of enquiring any further too exhausting to muster. She drifted to the sound of Riley zipping up a suit-case and woke again when she was gently being nudged.

'It's time to go,' Riley whispered. 'Our bags are in the car. Here, take these.' She handed her two pills again. 'I'll help you downstairs.'

Belle allowed herself to be guided out the door and down to the carpark. She hardly had the energy to ask if all her things had been packed, if anything had been left behind, if they shouldn't just try looking for Callum in a few more places before leaving. The desire to protest at all disintegrated before it reached her lips, her hurting body stealing every ounce of strength. She ached all over—her neck, her throat, her muscles, her eyes. As soon as she was in the car, she rested her head against the window, and because fighting the exhaustion was too insurmountable, she fell straight back to sleep again.

TWENTY

When Belle woke, she was in a quiet room on a comfortable bed beneath an eiderdown quilt. The pillow was soft, the shades drawn, and a tall glass of water and two pills lay beside her on the nightstand. There was something oddly familiar about the place, with its faint smell of sea air and damp, flames crackling gently in a fireplace on the opposite wall, a log splitting and falling behind the grate.

She tried to lift herself, but her head was heavy, and the room tilted. She collapsed back onto the pillow, her eyes gritty, like they were filled with sand. Her hands went immediately to her body and she felt the fabric of clean pyjamas there, and it all came back to her—arriving in Kircudbright, being half-carried up the stairs, and Riley changing her out of her clothes, tucking her into bed while Belle had been clammy with fever and only slightly lucid.

There was a soft knock at the door, then it opened a crack and a familiar face peered inside. 'Och, jolly good. You're awake.' Mrs Murray bustled in wearing an apron, a tea towel slung over one shoulder and a cup of tea in her hand. She walked to the bed, set the cup next to the water and pills and glanced down at her. 'Ye poor thing. Ye were so unwell when ye got here. Glad to see ye have a bit more colour in yer face now.'

'Mrs Murray.' Belle tried to sit up again but fell back, too exhausted to lift herself.

'Now, now, dinnae exert yerself. Ye have a rotten case of the flu. Never seen anyone look so peely-wally before. I'm glad Riley brought ye down here to recover. No chance at decent rest in that noisy Edinburgh hotel with only take-away food to eat.'

'How long have I been asleep for?'

'Ye arrived yesterday afternoon,' she said, 'and you've been asleep the whole night. It's mid-morning now.'

'I do feel a bit better,' she admitted. 'Just weak.'

'It's to be expected,' Mrs Murray said, smoothing down the quilt. 'Ye haven't eaten a thing in days. Take these.' She handed her the pills. 'It's proper flu relief. Then drink yer tea. I'll be back in a while with some hot chicken broth.'

She bustled out of the room and Belle curled into a ball, drifting back to sleep again.

When she came to, Mrs Murray had returned to her bedside with a tray. 'Dae ye feel like eating, lassie? I kin bring it back if ye want to sleep more.'

'No, no, I'll eat,' Belle said. The fever had broken at long last, and her stomach began to rumble. She worked her way into a sitting position as Mrs Murray set the tray on her lap. There was a bowl of steaming chicken broth with chunks of vegetables bobbing in the liquid, and slices of homemade bread on the side. 'It smells delicious.'

Mrs Murray beamed. 'You'll feel as good as new in no time.'

'It's been years since I've been this sick. Probably not since I was a child,' Belle said, taking a cautious spoonful of the broth. Although her throat was sore, the soup travelled down like silk, landing warmly in her stomach, rich and gently spiced.

'Well, I'm nae surprised,' Mrs Murray said, fussing around the bed, straightening the pillow and quilt. 'You've had an awful lot on yer plate, dear. What with losing yer father and now trying to find Callum. Riley told me ye weren't able to.' Her face fell. 'I'm truly sorry, lass. I'm sure Callum would have loved to have known ye.'

'We tried every place we could think of,' Belle said. 'We followed every crumb, asked every establishment with a kitchen, in so many towns. We even visited a cemetery because we'd been told he died.' She cast her eyes down at the soup. Then she'd fallen sick, just as they'd reached Edinburgh. And now, she was right back where she'd started, in Kirkcudbright.

Mrs Murray's hand was on hers. 'Dinnae be downcast, lassie. Callum will show up. Maybe not right away, but eventually he will, and we'll let him know about ye. He'll seek ye out, dinnae ye worry.'

'I just really wanted to find him. I wanted to be the one to tell him, to see that initial expression on his face, to know that he would want me in his life. I don't want to go home to wait and wonder.'

And yet, what choice did she have? Falling as ill as she had told her that she had endured enough over the past few months, the past year. It was time to rest, to let things be, to stop chasing ghosts and be kind to herself.

'Where's Riley?' she asked, dunking a slice of bread into the soup.

'She's gone out fur the day with Mr Murray to visit our art galleries.'

'Riley used to work in an art gallery for many years, in Sydney and in Rome.'

'Aye, she told us. Kirkcudbright is full of art. They won't be back fur hours. It'll give ye a chance to fully recover.' Mrs Murray smiled and placed her hand on Belle's forehead, checking for fever. 'You're nice and cool again, but I'd still prefer if our doctor dropped by and checked on ye.' When Belle went to object, she tut-tutted. 'Now, now, you're nae just a guest in my home, you're practically kin, and I won't take no fur an answer.'

LATER THAT AFTERNOON, as Belle was sitting up again with another bowl of hot broth, Riley poked her head through the door.

'Hey, you're awake,' she said, stepping into the room and sitting on the edge of the bed. 'How are you feeling?'

'Human again,' Belle said.

'You went downhill so quickly. I was going to call hotel reception for a doctor, but then I spoke to Mrs Murray and she said to bring you straight here.'

'I'm through the worst of it now.' Just a persistent sore throat and headache, but at least the fever had abated. And the doctor had visited, confirming she'd had a case of influenza but was on the mend. He'd prescribed fluids and rest, which Mrs Murray had nodded seriously at, as though making it her personal mission to fulfil.

'I'm sorry we didn't get to finish searching Edinburgh,' Riley said. 'I covered as many streets as I could while you were sleeping. Aside from one woman at a pub who directed me to a nursing home and another who had a toddler called Callum MacKenzie, I came up empty.'

Belle smiled her gratitude. 'It doesn't matter. We were never going to find him there. It was too big an area to search.'

'He'll turn up one day, and someone will mention his long-lost daughter was looking for him, and he'll come looking for *you*.'

'Maybe he'll turn Sydney upside down like we turned Scotland upside down.'

Riley laughed. 'Now *that* would be funny.'

'Did you enjoy the art?'

'I did. I met a few artists too. I like Kirkcudbright—the quiet. It's somewhere I could see myself living.'

'Well, don't get any ideas,' Belle chided. 'I'm not leaving you here.'

Riley laughed again. 'I booked our flights home. Day after tomorrow. I hope that's okay.'

Belle sighed with renewed defeat. 'Yes. I'm done. Disappointed but done.'

'We gave it our best shot, kid. No one can accuse us of anything less.'

'Maybe Mum was right. She said from the beginning that I should be content, that knowing Dad was enough. I should have listened to her. Despite our differences, our relationship was strong before he died.'

'Finding Callum was never about Edward not being enough.'

'I know,' Belle said. 'And I will always wonder about Callum. Maybe I'll even try to find him again. But right now, I don't have the energy for anything more than what we've already done.'

Riley stood and smoothed down her jeans. 'Can I get you anything? Tea, a stiff drink?'

Belle handed her the tray with the empty bowl. 'I might

sleep some more. I have one day left in Kirkcudbright without the stress of finding Callum. I want to enjoy it.'

Riley took the tray from her and smiled. 'I'm going to grab some dinner at the Selkirk. I'll drop by later to see how you are.'

'Have fun.'

She watched Riley leave before burrowing deep beneath the covers again and closing her eyes.

TWENTY-ONE

The next morning, the sun rose in a clear sky, lighting up the room, as Belle stretched and yawned. Her lungs were still congested, and she had a foggy head—the tell-tale signs of oversleeping—but her muscles weren't so weighted, and she had more energy.

She peeled back the covers and walked down the hall to use the shower, washing the sickness from her hair and skin, and brushing her teeth.

She dressed, then Mrs Murray knocked on the door as she was running her brush through her hair. The woman looked flustered, hands fluttering to her throat. 'Lass, some-one's just arrived fur ye downstairs.'

Belle put down the brush. 'Who?'

'I think ye should come see fur yerself.'

Belle pulled on her sneakers and followed Mrs Murray down the stairs into the dining room. As she entered, she saw Riley seated at the table with Mr Murray and another man, who was partially obscured from view. Riley turned in her chair and beamed at her, and the man glanced up, his intense blue gaze, so like her own, smacking her right in the core.

She inhaled sharply, her hand finding Mrs Murray's, who gripped her steadily.

The man rose and walked towards her. His hair, a similar shade to hers, like rich espresso, was peppered grey at the temples. He had a kind face and strong jaw, and long lashes framing those deep blue eyes.

It was like looking in the mirror.

'Belle,' he said, holding his hand out for her to shake. 'My name is Callum.'

For a moment, she could only stare, thoroughly caught, until she realised his hand was still outstretched and she took it in her own and shook it—her father's hand, wrapped around hers, after all this time. It was too wonderful and impossible and perplexing for words.

The room swayed a little. She was grateful for the reassuring presence of Mrs Murray, who was still standing beside her, a firm arm holding her steady.

'I've heard you've been looking fur me,' he said, his large, measuring eyes sweeping over her face. He was drinking her in too, quietly surveying.

'I have been,' Belle replied. Oh, how she knew those eyes. They were exactly like hers.

'Well, here I am.' He smiled. 'Shall we talk?'

'Yes,' she whispered.

───

THEY STROLLED TOGETHER, Callum leading her down to the river's edge near MacClellan's Castle, where scallop dredgers bobbed on the low tide and the breeze ruffled the water.

'This was one of my favourite spots as a bairn,' he said,

pausing at a retaining wall and hauling himself up to sit on it. He had a litheness that belied his age, an ease with which he scaled the wall. He'd obviously taken care of himself over the years, still fit and agile. 'We used to come down here at dawn and watch the fishing boats leave—Hamish, me, the other lads.' He inhaled deeply. 'It feels good to be back.'

Belle climbed up beside him and sat too. He had a pleasant Scottish brogue that she liked listening to. One that, strangely, felt like home. 'How long has it been since you were here?'

'Almost forty years. I left one day and never returned.' He glanced at her, then looked away.

'I guess Riley filled you in,' Belle said.

'Nae really. She said it wasn't her story to tell, that ye wanted to tell me yerself. But Hamish told me what he thought he knew—that ye were mine and ye were tracking me down.'

'Hamish was able to reach you?'

'Aye. Eventually. And Gilroy, Carlota, and my friend Eamon from the whisky emporium in Portree. I had dozens of voice messages by the time I got around to checking. They all said there were two young women looking fur me.'

Unbeknownst to her, as she'd turned Scotland upside down, news of her search for him had leaked like a sieve. Ironically, it wasn't he who had left the crumbs behind, but she, and Callum had followed them all the way.

'I'm glad you came,' she said. 'I thought all hope was lost, that I'd never find you.'

'We do share a likeness, lassie. So it's true, then? You're my daughter?'

The moment was almost too pivotal, too emotional, for her to answer properly. 'Yes,' she breathed. 'Yes, Callum. I'm your daughter.'

He blinked, then exhaled shakily, a stunned expression on his face. 'Well, I'll be damned.'

She watched as he ran a hand through his hair. She could have watched him for hours, discerning the similarities in their features, the likeness in their disposition. He had a warm manner and the same shaped mouth, and eyes so like hers it was as though she were staring at her reflection. When he caught her, she looked away, her cheeks flushing.

'I'm sorry. I'm still a little stunned,' he said sheepishly. 'I'm processing it slowly, but it's a lot to unpack. So yer Grace's daughter?'

'Yes.'

He whistled softly. 'She never told me about you. I had no idea ye existed.'

'She only realised she was pregnant when she returned home from Scotland,' Belle explained. 'She was engaged to my... dad. Edward. She didn't feel she had much of a choice other than to stay with him and let him raise me.'

'But she still should have told me. I wouldn't have turned her away,' he said firmly. 'I would have loved her. I would have loved ye both. I wish she'd known that.' His voice broke a little and he clasped his hands together, staring out at the river. 'Was he good to ye growing up? Edward, I mean. Was he a good father?'

'Yes,' she said without hesitating. 'Don't get me wrong, we had our differences. He wanted me to be a lawyer and I wanted to cook, so we didn't always see eye to eye. Most of the time I felt like I wasn't living up to his expectations. But it wasn't his fault. He carried the hurt of my mother's betrayal for a long time, and I was a constant reminder of that.'

'I'm sorry,' Callum said, sincerely. 'I knew yer mother

was engaged to someone while she was here. She was honest about it. But we were drawn to each other in a way that I've still never been able to fully comprehend. I'd love to say that I haven't thought about her much in the past years, but I can't. I still think about her every day.' He sighed and cast her a sad smile. 'Dae your parents know you're here?'

'Mum does,' Belle said. 'Dad died five weeks ago.'

'Och, lassie.' Callum looked devastated for her. 'I'm terribly sorry to hear that. He was a good man to have loved another man's child as his own. I'll never have the opportunity to thank him fur providing fur ye in the way that he did.' He slid his hands up and down the thighs of his jeans, strong and dexterous, bearing scars from the kitchen, like her own. He still seemed bewildered. 'And how is your mother? Is she well?'

'She's okay. Grieving, but okay.'

'Have ye known all yer life about me?'

Belle shook her head. 'No. I only found out about you when Dad died. As soon as I did, I came to find you. I'd always felt like a part of me was different or... missing. It made sense when Mum told me the truth.' She watched his expression as he digested her words. There was so much to catch up on, to tell each other.

'That's quite a secret to keep fur so long.' There was hurt and accusation in his voice, and Belle couldn't blame him. She understood what it meant to have your life turned on its head, to question the integrity of those you thought you knew. It was remarkable how well he was taking the news. Belle had tormented herself with images of rejection, of a door being closed in her face. The fact that he was sitting beside her, willing to listen, to allow her in, was testament to who he was.

The silence drew out, then he managed a smile. 'So, ye enjoy cooking?'

'I love it,' Belle answered.

'Me too. What dae ye like to cook?'

'Anything,' she said, 'but I love cooking Italian. I cooked in Rome for a year. Now I'm working in a little restaurant in Sydney called The Olive Grove.'

'I like cooking Italian too,' he said. 'Although I'm trained in French and Asian cuisine, while dabbling in molecular gastronomy. And of course, I make a mean haggis.'

Belle laughed. 'I'd love to try molecular gastronomy.'

'I could teach ye,' he said with a shy lift of his shoulder. 'I mean if ye would like me to.'

'Of course!' For some reason, her cheeks grew pink.

They shared a smile, his eyes holding hers for a moment.

'You know, you were quite hard to track down,' Belle said. 'We travelled from Kirkcudbright to Balloch to Broughty Ferry to Fort William, then on to Portree, Inverness and Edinburgh.'

His mouth fell open. 'Ye went to all those places looking fur me? You must have searched half of Scotland!'

'We did. We followed every lead, no matter how small. Even when we didn't have a lead, we just went to places, hoping you'd be there.'

He closed his eyes, releasing a dismayed breath. 'I'm so sorry. If only I'd known. I dinnae check my phone often. I work late and sleep most of the day, and to be honest, I'm nae used to people needing me. I'm nae married, and I dinnae have children, well, apart from you.' He gave a soft, shy laugh. 'I move from place to place frequently. I love trying different kitchens in different places, learning new skills. And I'm not one fur social media.'

'I would have kept searching,' Belle said defiantly. 'I wouldn't have stopped except I fell sick with the flu in Edinburgh and it brought the whole thing to an end.'

'Riley said ye were sick.' Concerned eyes swept over her. 'Are ye better now?'

'I am, but we didn't get to finish looking for you in Edinburgh.'

'It's just as well because I wasn't there.' His expression was both amused and apologetic. 'I was in Aberdeen, working in a restaurant.'

Belle could have kicked herself. 'We chose Edinburgh over Aberdeen! We thought you'd prefer the bigger city.'

He shrugged. 'I like all cities, all towns and villages. I'll drift anywhere my cooking takes me.'

'It didn't matter in the end. I would have got sick regardless and I probably wouldn't have found you in time.'

'Maybe it was meant to be,' he said. 'As soon as I found out ye were looking fur me, I came straight here. You and Riley wouldn't have arrived the day before if ye hadn't got sick.'

She grinned and stared out across the river, as the wind stirred the leaves of the tree above them. The guileless blue of the autumn sky and the jade-green hills beyond the water were so picturesque they could have been painted by an artist's brush. It was peaceful and hypnotic, as Belle breathed in the sea air and felt that final missing piece of her life slot into place. She was sitting on a wall beside her father, her *biological* father. He hadn't rejected her or the notion that she was his. He had a genuine interest in her, and she couldn't have asked for anything more from their first meeting.

'Are ye cold, lassie?' he asked as the breeze began to nip.

'A little, but I'm okay,' she said, burrowing down inside her jacket.

'You're still recovering from being sick. Let's get ye back to the Murrays' where it's warm.'

They hopped down off the stone wall and began the short journey back to Fable House.

'So, I was thinking,' he said, 'everyone's going to be blethering on once news of my long-lost daughter gets out. I'm sure Hamish has already told his wife, who's told her cousin, who's told her best friend, and probably the dog too.'

Belle laughed. 'Yes.'

'How about we eat in tonight? Just us and Riley and the Murrays, so we kin get to know each other properly.'

'Okay.'

'And I think,' he said, leaning in conspiratorially, 'that we kin convince Mrs Murray to let us cook in her kitchen. You and me. Making dinner. What dae ye say?'

Belle grinned widely. 'I say that's a fine idea.'

TWENTY-TWO

Callum set his knife roll bag on Mrs Murray's countertop, unfurling it to reveal a gleaming set of professional knives. Belle bent to inspect them—the large, rounded-tip blade of the chef's knife, the short and versatile paring knife, the long, jagged blade of the serrated knife. The handles were a rich, deep brown made of African blackwood that Belle instantly recognised as German-made.

'These are my Wüstoff knives. Forged steel,' Callum said, as though reading her mind. 'I have a Japanese set back in Aberdeen too, but my Germans are good fur hardier cooking when I'm nae so worried about precision slicing.'

'They're beautiful,' she said, running her fingertips along the handles. 'I have a knife set at home, but it's not as exceptional as this.'

'Would ye like to try one?' he asked.

'Really?' She'd never used a Wüstoff before, and she watched as he pulled the chef's knife from the bag and handed it to her, handle first.

'While ye were talking to Riley just then, I found some things in the fridge,' he said, as she inspected the knife, turning it over in her hands. 'Iona said we kin use it all, and I'll restock it fur her tomorrow. There's a rack of venison—we could roast it and serve it with whisky gravy and baked neeps. We could fry sprouts and black pudding fur a side dish too. We could make heather honey-roast carrots. Maybe even a salad with seared scallops. Although I dinnae think she's got scallops, and it might be too late to go down and buy them fresh. Never mind.' He waved his hands around animatedly, and she could see his brain imagining, creating, in the same way hers did when she dreamt up new menus. 'And fur dessert, we should do Clootie dumpling with Drambuie custard. Classic Scottish scran.'

She grinned at his passion, infectious and soul-warming, and she felt her blood pulse with the same energy. How long had it been since she'd cooked in a kitchen? Weeks. Edward's wake was the last time she'd prepared food, and just thinking of it caused heavy sorrow to grip her heart. She missed him. He was the only man she'd ever known as her dad, and although keeping Callum from her had been his idea, she knew he would have approved of this moment. Maybe not twenty or thirty years ago, but now, on this day, she was certain he would have let go of the past and embraced the future with her.

'Are ye okay?' Callum asked, touching her arm gently.

She swallowed the sadness away. 'I'm fine. Just a little tired.'

'We dinnae have to do this today,' he said quickly. 'You're still recovering. We kin cook tomorrow.'

She shook her head. 'It's okay. I want to stay.'

'Are ye sure?'

She'd spent so long searching for him that she wasn't about to let him out of her sight. 'Positive.'

'Well, I could start on the venison, and ye could do the

dessert. Then we can do the sides together. But if ye feel unwell at any time, go straight upstairs and lay down.'

'All right.'

He nodded, seeming satisfied that she would. 'Shall I write down the dumpling recipe fur ye?'

'You can just tell it to me. I'll remember.'

His sudden smile was full of pride. 'You're obviously very competent in the kitchen.'

'I've done a bit of *mise en place* before,' she joked.

'Ha!' He laughed. 'You're definitely my daughter.'

They stood side by side as he relayed the recipe for Clootie dumpling with Drambuie custard to her, and she committed it to memory before he returned to the fridge for the venison. She collected the suet and dry ingredients for the dumpling and placed them into a bowl.

'So, tell me about Rome,' Callum said, as he French-trimmed fat off the meat. 'I've nae been myself, but I've always wanted to cook in Italy.'

'I moved there a couple of years ago,' she explained, 'after my partner, Ben, ended our twenty-year relationship. Riley and I landed in Rome, and I worked in a tiny trattoria near Piazza Navona for a year. It was called Valentina's.'

'Did ye enjoy it?'

'I loved it. I didn't want to leave except I had an issue with a working visa and wasn't able to stay longer.' She still remembered how that visit from the immigration officials had sparked a chain reaction that had led them to Paris. 'My boyfriend still lives in Rome. His dad owns Valentina's. He came here for a few days to help us search for you.'

'Och, ye have a boyfriend. What's his name?'

'Andre.'

'So if you're based in Sydney, I take it you're doing long-distance.'

'Yes. But it's hard,' she admitted. 'Really hard.' Harder than she ever thought possible.

Callum smiled sympathetically. 'Those relationships usually are. But they're also worth fighting fur. Wouldn't ye have thrown in the towel by now if it wasn't?'

She nodded because she wanted so desperately for it to be true. 'Yes, I suppose.'

When he was finished trimming the venison, he patted it with olive oil and chopped parsley, thyme, and chives, dropping them into a food processor with gratings of gruyère and a nob of butter before blitzing them.

Along the countertop beside him, Belle made a well in a large bowl with her dry ingredients for the dumpling, whisking eggs and milk and adding them together. 'Carlota is an interesting woman,' she said, stirring in golden syrup to form a stiff mixture.

He glanced across at her as he pulsed the processor, and she wasn't sure he'd heard her until an embarrassed smile formed on his lips. 'I guess ye met my former girlfriend.'

'Yes. She was a little angry at us. She thought we'd replaced her.'

'Och dear.' He laughed out loud. 'Carlota is... well, Carlota. She's many things, and hot-headed is one of them.'

'I quite liked her,' Belle said, smiling too. She was teasing him as his cheeks grew pink.

'I met her in Broughty Ferry, and we lived together fur a short time,' he said with a shrug. 'But it wasn't meant to be. And I admit, I did leave her suddenly. She wasn't prepared fur it, and I can still feel the sting of her slap on my face when I told her I was leaving.'

'You left her because you didn't want children?' The question was out before she'd considered how inappropriate it was to ask. It was none of her business and yet, the idea of it had plagued her from the moment Carlota had told her.

He kept his eyes on the processor, although he'd ceased blitzing. 'She told ye that?'

'Yes.'

He let go of the processor and leaned back against the bench, finally meeting her eyes. 'I never not wanted children, Belle. If your mother had told me she was carrying my child, I would have wanted ye. But I'm almost sixty now. Do I want a newborn at this age? No, I dinnae. I won't lie. But in my twenties and thirties, of course I wanted a family.' He wiped his hands on a tea towel and turned back to the processor, pulling the lid off and spooning the herb mixture out onto the venison. 'I guess settling down wasn't on the cards fur me. And so, I worked in lots of different kitchens and made a name fur myself in the industry instead.

'As fur Carlota, she was never the woman fur me. I feel bad fur the way I hurt her, but she'll find someone else, I'm sure. She has a lot of love to give.' He grimaced slightly. 'Sorry, lassie. This must make you squeamish, listening to yer father talk about women.'

'No, it's fine,' Belle said, blushing slightly.

'Aye. I guess I'm not really yer da so it's nae the same. Ye had a proper da, one who loved ye all yer life.' His expression grew pensive.

'And I loved him too, but he's gone, and he's handing the reins over to you now.' Something she firmly believed.

'I want to be angry with her,' Callum said softly. His hands paused in their work on the venison. 'Your mother, I mean. I want to know why she, why *they*, stole my time with you.' He sighed heavily, before glancing at her. 'It's time we'll never get back. What gave them that right?'

Belle nodded solemnly. 'I know. But she was frightened. And she has so many regrets. That doesn't excuse what she did. She should have told you, but she was afraid.'

'Maybe that's why I can't find it in my heart to hate either of them. Maybe I understand why they did it. Maybe I still love her in spite of it.' He blinked and Belle saw the emotion in his eyes, heard the thickness in his voice.

'Is that why you never settled down?' she asked.

His brow furrowed as if trying to ascertain how best to answer. 'Aye. No. Probably. I dinnae know.' He smiled reluctantly. 'I've never met anyone I've wanted to stand still with. I made cooking my passion instead and that's what's filled my life.'

'And now?' Belle's voice was full of hope that he'd have room for his daughter.

'Let's just say my life in Aberdeen is nae going to be the same,' he replied. 'I dinnae know how it could be, knowing what I know now. I have a daughter.' He chuckled, his shoulders shaking with renewed disbelief. 'I have a *daughter*!'

They whiled the rest of the afternoon away in comfortable conversation. They laughed at the same things and Callum seemed genuinely interested in her stories. As he slid the venison into the oven and she fired up the stove to simmer the dumpling, she told him of her childhood, and he asked questions about Ben and Andre and Riley, about her time at school, and the moment she had realised she loved to cook.

'Considering Mum can burn water and my dad never once set foot inside the kitchen, it was a wonder I knew how to cook at all,' she joked.

'It was in yer blood, lassie,' he said with a proud,

lopsided grin. 'It was always in yer blood. And if there was one thing I could have given ye as your father, I'm glad it was that.'

TWENTY-THREE

Later that night, they sat down to eat with the Murrays and Riley, a low fire crackling behind the grate. Tumblers of whisky glowed copper in their hands, and there was the glorious chink of cutlery against china as platters of venison, heather honey-roast carrots, and fried sprouts with discs of black pudding were passed around. It reminded Belle of the staff dinners at Valentina's, a pang of homesickness for Andre and Rome stabbing at her chest.

'Ye must be exhausted,' Mrs Murray said to her, eyes narrowing with concern. 'You've not long recovered and ye went to all this trouble to cook fur us.'

'I didn't do much,' Belle said, smiling at Callum.

He shook his head, wiping the corners of his mouth with a napkin. 'She's telling fibs. She did quite a bit. Put me to shame, frankly.'

Belle laughed and sipped her whisky. She *was* tired, her muscles lethargic and her eyes heavy, but she couldn't have gone to sleep if she tried. She wanted to remain at the table and learn everything there was to learn about Callum—not his life story, but the little things that made him *him*. What he thought about certain topics, what made him happy or sad, his favourite food to eat and, more importantly, where she would fit into his life. She didn't want to rush things or scare him away—they were both still processing the enormity of it—but she was leaving for home the next day and there was so little time left to recoup what they'd lost.

After dinner, Mrs Murray and Callum cleared the dishes away, then everyone sat around the fire, hands folded around their tumblers as Callum told them stories of his travels around Scotland and the kitchens he'd worked in. Curled up on the lounge beside him, Belle hung on his every word and occasionally, he glanced across at her and their eyes held, and he'd smile the most contented smile, still imbued with incredulity. But he seemed happy, and she was so grateful for that because the alternative was too sad to contemplate.

At midnight, her eyes began to close and she could no longer fight the exhaustion.

'Bedtime for ye,' Callum said, in a firm, fatherly way. 'Before ye fall asleep in yer whisky.' He stood and helped her to her feet, taking her tumbler and placing it down on the coffee table.

As they headed to the staircase, she asked, 'Are you staying here also?'

'I am.'

'Then I'll see you tomorrow morning at breakfast before our flight?'

'Ye will.' He smiled softly, eyes shiny from the drink, an expression of disbelief still stamped on his face. 'I just can't believe after all this time...' He seemed to hesitate, and she wasn't sure if a hug was appropriate, so she touched his arm gently and he blinked, tears welling in his eyes.

'Goodnight,' she said.

He sniffed. 'Aye. Sleep well.'

Riley followed her up the stairs and together they walked to Belle's room.

When they reached her door, Belle's hand stilled on the handle, and she turned to face her friend. 'I've been thinking...'

'That you don't want to leave tomorrow.'

Belle grimaced. 'Is it that obvious?'

'You've just found Callum,' Riley said, as though the idea of leaving now was preposterous. And it was.

Belle broke into a grin. 'Yeah, I did.' The knowledge of it still floored her. 'Will you stay with me, just for a few extra days, then we can fly home together?'

'Well, I'm not about to fly home without you. Will work let you have the extra time off?'

While Belle had been unwell, Carlo had left her another message, asking her when she'd be returning to work. Her father had died almost five weeks ago, and all the leave Carlo had given her was already up. Life was calling her back, and she *would* return, but she needed a few more days. 'I'll call Carlo in the morning. I'll explain everything. I'm sure he'll understand.'

Riley nodded, then opened the door to her room. 'I'm glad you found your dad. He seems nice.'

'Yes,' Belle agreed. 'He is.'

BELLE WOKE to the pitter-patter of rain on the roof. She opened her eyes and stretched, taking a moment to gather her thoughts, the day before playing back like a slideshow. *Callum*. Had it all been a dream? Had she wanted to find him so badly that she'd imagined meeting him?

She smiled. No. He'd been as real as the sun in the sky and just as wonderful. When she'd thought all hope was lost, he'd arrived, like the calm after a storm.

She pushed back the covers and swung her legs over the side of the bed, toes touching the cold boards. Sleep had come swiftly after a long day and more than a few tots of whisky, and she'd hardly moved all night, not even to dream of Ben or Avery or Paris.

She stood, her lungs and head clear, her throat better, deciding the whisky had definitely helped. She walked to the window and pushed the curtain aside. The sky was grey, silvery darts of rain falling, puddles pooling by the side of the road and the occasional passing car sending a spray of water whooshing up.

Beyond her closed door, Fable House was quiet, and she dressed, pulling her hair into a ponytail before splashing water on her face and brushing her teeth in the bathroom. Riley's door was open as she passed it, but her bed was made and the room empty, so Belle trotted down the stairs and into the dining room.

It was empty too, save for Callum sitting by the fire with his laptop balanced on his knees. He glanced up at her approach, eyes crinkling with warmth. 'Good morning.'

'Morning.'

'Did ye sleep well?'

'I'm not sure I moved once my head hit the pillow.'

'Aye, you've been asleep fur a while.'

'What time is it?' She hadn't checked her phone or watch before coming down. She'd assumed, given the dull colours outside, that it was early morning.

'Almost lunch.'

Belle flushed. 'I'm so sorry. You should have woken me up.'

Callum closed his laptop. 'I would dae no such thing. Ye needed the sleep, lassie. And you're better for it, I kin tell. Hungry?'

She was famished. 'Yes.'

'I'll make ye some breakfast. My famous apple, maple syrup and almond porridge to warm your belly.'

She followed him into the kitchen and watched as he placed oats and milk in a large saucepan on the stove. 'Where is everyone?' she asked.

'Riley mentioned that she rescheduled your flights for later in the week, so the Murrays took her fur a drive to visit some of the castles around Dumfries and Galloway. There are quite a few.'

She glanced out the window at the rain.

Callum looked up from the pot on the stove to follow her gaze. 'The weather's nae great, but it's going to move on soon. I thought once it cleared, we could go fur a walk.'

Belle nodded. 'I'd love that.'

She ate her porridge in the dining room, soul-warming as she knew it would be, with the crunch of almonds and the crisp sweetness of the apples. Callum sipped coffee and watched her with anticipation, the way every cook does when they set a meal down in front of someone, hoping and praying that they love it. She'd worn that same look many times.

'There's a cooking expo in Glasgow in three days' time,' he said, setting his mug down on the table. 'Since you're going to be here, I thought...'

She swallowed a mouthful of porridge. 'Yes!'

'Really? You'd like to go with me?' He broke into a surprised but pleased grin. 'That makes me happy indeed. I'll purchase some tickets for us.'

She grinned too.

When she finished eating, he beamed delightedly at her empty bowl, then swooped it off the table, disappearing into the kitchen to wash and dry it.

The rain was finally easing and the clouds clearing. Callum returned and Belle rose from the table. 'Thank you for making me breakfast. It was the best porridge I've ever tasted.'

'Ah.' He waved his hand as though it were nothing at all, but he'd missed many opportunities to cook his child a meal and she could see the significance of the moment in his expression.

'I might make a couple of quick calls before we head out,' she said. 'Do you mind?'

'Not at all,' he said. 'I have a few things left to do. I'll see ye back down here when you're ready.'

She took the stairs two at a time, and returned to her room, closing the door behind her. Locating her phone on the nightstand, she dialled her mother's number.

'We found him,' Belle said, after Grace answered.

There was a stunned gasp on the other end of the line, followed by her mother's trembling voice. 'You found him?'

'Well, technically, he found us,' she replied. 'Seems *we* were the ones leaving a trail.' She explained how they'd arrived in Edinburgh after failing to find him in Portree or Inverness, and how she'd become unwell with the flu. 'I was bedridden, and Riley brought me back to Kirkcudbright, to the Murrays. Callum had heard we'd been searching for him and arrived here the following day.'

'You found him,' her mother repeated, a whisper this time, laced with surprise and something else. Trepidation.

'He's wonderful, Mum, just like you said he was. We've got to know each other a bit. Obviously, we still have a long way to go.'

'Does he... I mean, does he remember me?' Grace's tone was uncertain.

'Of course he remembers you,' Belle said gently. 'I don't think he ever forgot you.'

'And you told him? Everything? About what I did?'

'Yes.'

A soft, quivering sigh. 'He must hate me.'

'He doesn't hate you, Mum. He's just... it was a lot for him to take in. It still is.'

Her mother made a scoffing noise. 'Don't sugarcoat it. I took away his right to know his child, to meet you and love you. I wouldn't blame him for hating me.'

Belle could hear her steely resolve crumble. 'It was a decision you and Dad made together. You had your reasons.'

'Reasons or not, what we did was inexcusable.' Grace's voice broke. 'And Callum always was too kind.'

'I'm not sure there's any point to this,' Belle said, 'beating yourself up. What's done is done. The main thing is we found him.'

'But I'm deeply ashamed. I always have been. More than you'll ever know.' Grace began to cry, all the hurt and grief and regret of the past weeks and years spilling out over that call.

'Mum...' Belle's heart broke, and she wished she was there to hug her, to show her that she'd been forgiven in a way that would mean more than words over the phone. Decisions made a lifetime ago, when Grace had been young and scared and lonely, may not have been the right ones, but hindsight was a fearsome gift. It was full of reflection and regret, entirely bittersweet, and always a lesson learned too late.

'I suppose the good to come of this is that as a daughter,

you filled Edward's life when children weren't possible for him, and now you'll fill Callum's. And that's some consolation.' Grace sniffed through her tears.

'I'm not sure where we'll go from here, whether he'll want me in his life. We haven't really spoken about it yet, but I think he will.'

'I know time was taken from you and everything must feel urgent now but try to take it day by day.'

Belle agreed. The last thing she wanted was to impose on Callum or make him feel that his comfortable life needed changing. She'd spent her whole life disappointing the men she loved and the last thing she wanted to do was send him running.

They spoke a little more, then ended the call shortly after, Belle promising to be home within the week. As she hung up, another idea began forming in her mind, and she quickly dialled Andre.

He would be on the lunch shift at Valentina's and while she hoped he'd hear his phone behind the bar, it rang through to his voicemail, so she left a message.

'I have so much to tell you,' she began. 'We found Callum! Well, he kind of found us. But he's wonderful! And we're back in Kirkcudbright, and we'll be heading home soon. Before we fly to Sydney, can you spare a day or two in London? Or I'll come closer to you—Munich or Nice or Vienna.' She was rambling, for there was so much to tell him. 'I don't want this to be all we have for the next year. Please... please meet me. I miss you more than I can bear sometimes.' His mailbox cut her off with a resounding beep and, feeling deflated, with so much more that she wanted to ask him, she closed her eyes and sighed.

Would her life with Andre ever become easier? Or would they forever be resigned to that disheartening dance of missed calls and text messages? The love two people felt for each other wasn't always conducive to a successful relationship. Sadly, she was beginning to realise that love was only part of the equation. It needed more to keep the foundations from collapsing, like closeness and touch and whispers in the middle of the night.

Love... it hadn't been enough for Callum and her mother, or for Riley and Leo, and she worried that it wasn't going to be enough for her and Andre. Her heart grew sick at the thought, but she tried her hardest to ignore it for now. A whole afternoon with her father awaited and she didn't want it to be tainted by her sadness.

She made one last call, this time to Carlo, to explain her absence, but she was forced to leave a message when he didn't answer. Then she dropped her phone into her bag, climbed to her feet, and headed back downstairs.

TWENTY-FOUR

The rain finally cleared and cold light pushed through the clouds to shine on Kirkcudbright. Belle and Callum were on a walking trail that had started at Harbour Square, leading them to a track called Sailor's Walk, which they followed along the shoreline of the River Dee and around St Mary's Isle.

The woodland was deciduous and enchanting, leaves carpeting the trail, soggy and glistening from the wet weather. As they navigated a path surrounded by lichen-covered trees and wild purple rhododendrons, Belle imagined it was the sort of place fairies and nymphs would inhabit, their tiny bodies and wispy wings glittering in the undergrowth, sparkling at dusk.

From the Point of the Isle, Callum pointed to a view of Kirkcudbright Bay through the trees, framed by wooded shores, with the lighthouse guarding the mouth of the estuary.

'I used to ride my bike all through these trails as a wee bairn,' he said. 'Maybe one day you'll bring yer children to bonnie Scotland, and they'll make memories of their own.

Ye kin share stories of yer ancestors and culture long after I'm gone and you're the only one left to tell them.'

The idea of it was dispiriting, for children, once a dream Belle had thought entirely within her grasp, seemed less and less likely these days, especially with Andre so far away. It filled her with immense sorrow.

At her silence, Callum cleared his throat apologetically. 'I hope I haven't upset ye, lassie.'

She shook her head. 'No, it's just...' She sighed. It was what it was—Andre and all the things that would likely never be. She couldn't hope to put it into words and smiled bravely instead. 'Yes, maybe one day.'

He returned the smile, then indicated with his hand that they should continue walking. They rounded the rocky shoreline of John Paul Jones's Point as the cry of the curlew pierced the air.

'I recall Mrs Murray mentioned that your parents had passed on,' Belle said.

'Aye.' He nodded. 'Yer biological grandparents are gone now, but I have an older brother and two younger sisters, all scattered around Scotland. They'd love to meet ye, the niece they never knew about.'

'I've never had aunties, uncles or cousins before.' That she'd seen often anyway. Her mother was an only child too, and her father's family lived regionally and interstate, so she hardly saw them. 'I became aware of your sister Lainey while looking for you. We thought she might have been in Inverness, but we couldn't find her.'

'Aye, Lainey. My youngest sister. She lives outside Inverness, actually. She's a nurse at a royal infirmary.'

It explained why Belle hadn't been able to locate her. She hadn't called any hospitals outside Inverness and none that were royal infirmaries.

'Are ye an only child or did yer parents have other children?' he asked. They were back on the forest path, wildfowl calling from the pebbly beaches beyond the trees, the air perfused with the scent of the salty sea.

'I'm an only child,' she explained. 'My dad—Edward—couldn't have children.'

Callum's face fell with genuine sadness. 'I'm sorry to hear that. What a difficult situation fur ye all.'

'It was a little lonely growing up,' she admitted. 'A sibling would have been nice, and it would have taken the pressure off me too.' It was easy talking to him, even about such things as Edward, which was surprising, given the circumstances. 'Dad always had high hopes that his only child would study law. It wasn't ever clear to me why I didn't want to, why I wasn't like him. Up until I found out about you, I just thought something was wrong with me.'

Callum nodded, imperceptible tilts of his head indicating he was listening. He seemed thoroughly engrossed in all she had to say and likewise, she hung on his every word.

'Anyway, it was nice to have Riley around when I was a teenager, and I met Ben when we were both sixteen. He was a lawyer too and the apple of Dad's eye.' She smiled at the memory, never with jealousy, for she'd always loved their relationship.

'Yer father's death must have broken Ben's heart.'

Her smile slipped and a familiar ache squeezed her chest. 'Actually, Ben died the year before. It was *his* death that broke my father's heart.'

'Och.' Callum scrubbed at his jaw, understanding dawning on his face. 'How did he die?'

She hadn't intended to bring Paris up, to cloud such a beautiful day with her father, but it had become a significant part of her life and there was no way to explain most things without it. So she told him of her dash from Rome and the immigration officials, fleeing to Paris with Riley, of Ben arriving at her hotel door at the same time Andre and Avery were checking in downstairs, and of taking Ben for a drink to say goodbye at the Papilles Café, only to find themselves trapped in the darkest nightmare she could ever have imagined.

Her cheeks were wet when she finished talking, and she wasn't sure when the tears had come, but they were there, scurrying down her cheeks. She wasn't over Paris. It still trapped her in its torment—the gunfire, Ben's body bleeding out on her lap, the stillness and the cries and the torturous waiting to hear if Riley, Andre, and Avery were alive. To lose Avery, a young and spirited soul with everything to live for.

They had arrived at the end of the walk, back at Harbour Square, their starting point, and Callum pointed to a café. There was still so much to talk about—of love and Paris and loss, of the future and how they moved forward, and she wanted to talk about Andre too. To gain an outsider's perspective on what she felt so surely in her heart might be the beginning of the end, for he hadn't returned any of her calls.

Callum placed his hand on her shoulder, and she nodded at the café. Yes. A coffee would be nice, for they still had a whole afternoon together and a lifetime to catch up on.

SAYING goodbye to the Murrays was surprisingly difficult. It was odd, really, that in a matter of weeks, Belle had come to love them like family, and although she no longer had living grandparents on Callum's side, the Murrays had become a delightful, unexpected substitute. Their warm home and even warmer embrace had provided a haven and harbour to anchor to when all else had felt desolate.

Belle's eyes filled with tears, and she heard Mrs Murray sniff back her own soggy emotion.

'Ye be safe now, won't ye?' she declared, hugging Belle, then releasing her to press Riley to her bosom. 'Safe flight home and all. Dae come back. You've got Kirkcudbright blood in yer veins!'

'We'll be back,' Belle said with a certainty that made Riley nod with agreement.

They each took a turn hugging Mr Murray, who was slightly less emotional, but no less sombre to see them leave.

'And dinnae ye be a stranger either.' Mrs Murray wagged her finger at Callum. 'Fur goodness' sake, ye can't let thirty-eight years go by before we see ye again.'

Callum squinted up the high street of his childhood town and smiled. 'Maybe I'll come home now. I've had enough of travelling. And I have a reason to be back, to set up somewhere permanent.' His smile grew and he directed it at Belle. 'We can't have ye traipsing all over Scotland looking fur me next time.'

She flushed, laughing. Perhaps it *had* been a bold move to scour all of Scotland for a man whose name was like a thousand others, but it had yielded the outcome she'd hoped for. More than she'd hoped for.

They waved goodbye to the Murrays. The sound of Mrs Murray blowing her nose into a hanky trailed them up the street as they walked to the hire car, located a few spots from Callum's.

'See ye in Glasgow,' he called back to them as he

continued to his car, a duffel bag slung over his shoulder and his knife roll bag in the other hand.

Riley settled behind the wheel, and they followed him out of Kirkcudbright as the sun emerged from the morning's mist to splay across green pastures and deeply rolling valleys. Scotland was as diverse as she was beautiful, with her towering mountains and dark forests, her placid lochs and stunning coastlines. In some ways, it made Belle homesick for Australia and in other ways, she felt like she *was* home. She thought about what awaited her in Sydney—a job she liked but that was distracting rather than fulfilling, a social life that was trepidatious, a love who was always too far from her.

She had much to be grateful for—Andre, her mother, Riley, Callum, the fact that she was alive—but a lot of it was disjointed and not quite whole, as though each aspect was missing some fundamental thread that pieced it all together. She'd hoped finding Callum would be binding, like an adhesive, but it wasn't, not entirely, and she knew what she was still missing—Andre. Without him, nothing would truly feel whole again.

They reached Glasgow two hours later and Riley navigated the rental car behind Callum's into a hotel carpark. Belle had just over twenty-four hours left with her father and hopefully, if the stars aligned, an impromptu visit with Andre somewhere on the Continent before she returned to her life. If he ever called her back, anyway.

TWENTY-FIVE

Before leaving the hotel for the cooking expo the next day with Callum, Belle tried calling Andre again. The time was appropriate, just after breakfast in Rome when she knew he'd be getting ready for work or maybe walking there. But several attempts failed to reach him, his voicemail answering every time.

She tried not to read too much into it. He was busy and hadn't heard his phone, still on silent from the night before. Maybe he had the day off and was sleeping. She knew so much about him and yet sometimes so little, all the intricacies of his daily life constantly evolving so they'd become a mystery. She didn't want to acknowledge that maybe he'd chosen *not* to answer, that their time in Scotland had cemented in his mind what she'd been most afraid of, that fragments of togetherness was too lonely a way forward, and that a girl in Rome could offer less complication.

She held no resentment, just a deep and utter sadness, a longing to speak to him one last time, to hear him say it was over, so she knew for sure, to hold him and be held before they said goodbye.

The cooking expo was an ideal distraction, stalls show-casing the latest technology in cookware and appliances, and hosting demonstrations of new knife sets and frypans. There was food and wine and produce for sale, and almost every stall offered a taste of what they'd prepared using their cookware—little cups of fried fish and wagyu beef, and small squares of focaccia and chocolate cake. It was packed inside, people brimming and jostling, and at times, far too crowded.

After a few hours roaming the stalls, they sat down to lunch at an outdoor table beneath an umbrella, Callum choosing a char kway teow from a Malaysian kiosk and Belle selecting a vibrant, spicy paella from the Spanish one.

Riley had foregone the expo, spending the day at the Kelvingrove Art Gallery and Museum instead, where she no doubt revelled in the quiet, unlike the bustle of the expo, which made Belle's nerves prickle.

'I've noticed you're pretty jumpy in crowds, lass,' Callum said, dragging his fork through his noodles. His tone held no accusation, just curiosity and concern. 'Riley too. Last night at that restaurant her eyes were darting all over the place. Is that because of Paris?'

Belle shrugged, trying to push down the emotion that welled whenever anyone spoke of Paris, and she was forced to confront it. 'It's a habit we haven't quite kicked yet.'

'It's called post-traumatic stress.' His words were kind, his tone soft.

'It's nothing.' She glanced back inside the exhibition centre, knowing it wasn't nothing at all. It had become a force unto itself. It had become everything.

'Dae ye think it would be worth seeing someone just in case this nothing turns into something?' He wouldn't let it go, gently persisting.

She frowned at him. 'You sound like Mum.'

His smile was wry. 'Well, at least we're aligned on some things.'

She watched him closely, studying his expression. 'You don't hate her, do you? For what she did.'

He sighed, staring down at his plate of food. It took him a few moments to answer. 'No, lass. I dinnae hate her. Hate is a powerful thing, and I dinnae have it in me. But she broke my heart, first when she left me thirty-eight years ago, and second when our daughter showed up looking fur me.' His forehead crinkled, as though trying to fend off unwanted hurt. 'I won't pretend to like what she did, fur I'll never get back those years with ye. But in some small way, I kin understand. At least, I'm trying to.'

'She wants your forgiveness. I hope someday you can give it to her.'

'In time it will come, I'm sure.' He smiled reassuringly, even if his eyes said otherwise. If not by experience, then by parental instinct, he was trying to make her feel better.

After lunch, they ventured back into the expo, but they didn't linger, just long enough for Callum to buy a Dead Sea salt set, bottles of oil and vinegar from Modena, and a new cherry pitter. 'I left mine at Carlota's by mistake,' he explained with a chuckle. 'I've been too afraid to ask fur it back.'

Belle had her eye on several different knives, but the intricate problem of airport customs made the purchase impossible, so she settled on two cookbooks that would store easily in her bag. Then they left, bound for the hotel again and the last of their time together.

THE FLIGHT HOME departed in the early afternoon, which gave Belle a few hours to attempt reaching Andre again in the hope that they'd be able to see each other before she left. But as had been the case the previous two days, she was unable to reach him. This time, his phone was off, diverting straight to voicemail, and the significance of that couldn't have been plainer. She'd left several messages and he'd had ample opportunity to call her back or text at least. He hadn't and that spoke volumes.

Her regret, and she had many, was that he hadn't talked to her about it, to explain why, even though she knew all too well the challenges they faced. She would have understood. She would have been devastated—she *was* devastated—but she would have understood. Long-distance was agonising. It was torturous and draining and uncertain. It left them both heartsick, but simply falling silent and refusing to speak to her was equally as torturous, and not what she would have done to him.

She tried not to let it mar her final moments with Callum, as they stood by the entrance to customs.

'I wanted to buy ye something at the expo,' he said, a fond grin on his face, 'but then I thought, maybe I could give ye something that's brought me a lot of joy over the years.' From a grey satchel looped across his torso, he pulled a tattered notebook out, spiral-bound, bursting with pages, some that were loose and folded neatly inside. Colour touched his cheeks as he handed it to her. 'It was my mam's. Her recipe keeper. She never went anywhere without it.'

Belle took the notebook and carefully opened the cover. The first page was blank, except for a name scrawled at the top. *Maggie MacKenzie's Recipes*.

'That was my mam. Your biological grandmother,' Callum explained. 'Every recipe she ever learned she wrote down in that book or wrote it on a piece of paper and kept it in there—all the Scottish classics and others too.'

Belle thumbed gently through the pages, recipes for haggis and tattie scones, Cullen skink and Scottish stovies jumping from the pages. There were other recipes too, for pork pie, beef stew and Yorkshire pudding. Sometimes Maggie had accompanied the method with a hand-drawn sketch of what she'd thought the finished dish should look like. She had been a clever illustrator in a time when glossy cookbooks were uncommon.

Belle's heart tripped with gratitude. The gift was impossibly kind but too much for her to accept, for it was obvious how much this book meant to Callum.

She shook her head. 'I can't take this from you.' She handed it back to him.

He smiled, gently returning it to her. 'Ye can and ye will. I won't take no fur an answer. She would want ye to have it.' He shrugged. 'Besides, I've memorised every recipe in it.'

'But this is special to you—a precious keepsake. You can't possibly give it away.'

'I'm nae giving it away,' he said firmly. 'I'm handing it down to ye, the way it was handed down to me.' He pointed to the back cover. 'There are some blank pages at the end. It would make me proud if ye would add some of yer recipes next to a few of mine.'

Emotion coiled in her throat, and she could barely swallow past it, as she stared down again at the notebook. 'I don't know what to say.'

'Say you'll take it and use it and love it.'

'I'll do all of those things.' A tear scampered down her cheek and she hastily wiped it away. 'Maggie loved to cook.'

'Did she ever,' Callum pronounced. 'She was the one

who taught me. And it looks like she inadvertently taught you too.'

Belle held the notebook close to her chest, mourning a past that was lost to her, decisions that could never be unmade, and people she would never know. But time had also given her a new path, the chance to know the ones who remained, a future that gleamed more hopefully.

Riley touched her arm. 'We'd better go. We've still got to get through customs.'

Callum drew himself up, as though bracing himself for the goodbye. 'I hate to see ye leave, lassie. We just found each other.'

'I'll be back soon,' she said with conviction.

'Maybe I could come to Sydney. Would ye mind?'

'I'd love that!'

He grinned, then stepped forward, hesitantly holding out his arms. 'I'll never be able to thank ye enough fur coming here, fur seeking me out with such determination. Ye dinnae know what it means to me.' His breath caught on the last words and his jaw trembled.

Her resolve crumbled and that single treacherous tear from earlier turned into a gulping stream. He pulled her close and hugged her, patting her back. 'There, now lass. Dinnae cry. We have so much to look forward to.'

She sniffed tearily into his shoulder. 'Yes, we do.'

They parted and he patted her arm. 'Have a safe flight. Call me when ye get home, so I know you're okay.'

'I will.' She clutched Maggie's notebook close, collected the handle of her luggage and waved goodbye to Callum. Then they rounded the door to customs, and he disappeared from view.

On the plane, as they waited for take-off, Belle checked

her phone for a return call from Andre before switching it off for the flight.

'Still can't get a hold of him?' Riley asked, glancing at her.

Belle shook her head. 'No. I'll try again when I'm home, just to know where his head is at, if he'll answer me.'

Riley's glum smile said it all. It was an opportunity lost, one last chance for them to reunite briefly again in Europe before Belle left for Sydney, if only to understand why Andre had gone quiet. She was owed that much at least. She tried not to let the insult surface, instead focusing her thoughts on Callum and what their new relationship would bring. Edward was gone now, but in return, as though he were repenting for his sin, she had been given her biological father. Not a replacement, but a continuation.

And although she was going home and that filled her with uncertainty, she had found other ties too—in Scotland, with a father who, despite only knowing for a few days, she'd forged an immediate bond with. Steady and durable. Quietly everlasting. The bond between parent and child that was as old as the world itself, no matter the absent years in between.

TWENTY-SIX

The plane touched down in Sydney on a bright spring morning, the sun already high in the sky. Belle and Riley disembarked and passed uneventfully through customs and quarantine, discovering Grace in the arrivals concourse, waiting for them.

'Mum?' Belle walked directly to her, and they hugged. 'I didn't know you were going to meet us here.'

'I wanted to surprise you,' she said. 'How was the flight?' She looked better than she had when Belle had left three weeks earlier. Colour had returned to her gaunt cheeks and her hair was styled again, her clothes smoothly pressed. She still held a deep sadness in her eyes, a tranquil sorrow in the tilt of her head, but she wore her grief and the lies of the past with quiet resolve and apology.

'Fine. Tiring,' Riley said, hugging her too. 'It's good to see a familiar face.'

They dragged the luggage from the concourse out to the carpark. The air was hot when they stepped outside, the sun fierce in a cobalt sky. Belle was quick to yank off her jacket.

Riley flicked her head towards the taxi rank. 'This is where I'll say goodbye.'

On the plane, Belle had offered her a spare room at her place until Riley decided her next move, and she was surprised to see her assessing the line of taxis. 'No way,' she said emphatically. 'You're not catching a taxi and you're not staying in a hotel. You're coming home with me, remember?'

Riley smiled. 'You two have a lot to talk about. I'll only get in the way. Besides, I'm flying back to Perth tomorrow.'

'You're leaving already?' Belle's world tilted again.

'Yes.'

Belle rushed forward and embraced her. 'But you can't leave now,' she whispered into Riley's shoulder. 'I'm not ready to lose you again.' If their time in Scotland had taught her anything, it was that neither of their worlds spun properly without the other in it.

Riley held her close, her arms circling her protectively. 'I have a feeling I'll be back soon. Then you won't be able to get rid of me.'

'I wish that was my problem.' Belle pulled away, smiling. 'Thank you for coming with me, for helping me find Callum.'

'I wouldn't have been anywhere else, kid.' Riley swiped a tear from her eye and sniffed disapprovingly at it. She straightened, collected the handle of her suitcase, gave them a mock salute, then turned and walked towards the taxi rank.

Belle watched her leave, trying to stem the threat of tears as well, her heart heavy with all the goodbyes she'd had to endure over the last few days. She stayed there watching until Riley was in a taxi, waving from the back window.

'Ready to go?' Her mother's hand was on her arm.

Belle nodded solemnly and followed her through the airport carpark to the car. After stowing Belle's luggage in the boot, they climbed in, and Grace navigated them onto Qantas Drive and to her house, where Belle's car was still parked.

'You're welcome to stay with me,' she said, guiding them through morning peak-hour traffic. 'I'd love the company.'

'Thanks, but I have to get back to work,' Belle explained. 'Unless you *need* me to stay.' She thought of her dad's office and his clothes in the wardrobe, all the things that would eventually need to be packed away when the time was right, and how she wanted to be there for her mother when that time came.

Grace waved her hand. 'No, you go home, sweetheart. I'm sure work would like you back soon.'

They fell silent and Belle's jetlagged thoughts drifted to Andre, her heart still bruised. She'd tried to push him from her mind on the plane ride home, but there was no avoiding what was to come—the time to mourn everything that was lost. They would talk again, she was sure, for they couldn't leave it all unsaid, but it was a conversation she wasn't looking forward to.

'Callum would like to come visit,' she said. It was as much to distract herself as it was to address the other unsaid thing—her biological father. 'Maybe not right now, but someday.'

Grace swallowed but remained silent.

'Would you mind if he did?'

She glanced at Belle, then back at the road, and it was a long time before she answered. 'I'm sure he'd be coming for you, not me.'

'He'll want to see you too. It's been a long time and you need to talk.'

Grace fell silent again.

'He doesn't want to be angry at you, but he needs to heal also,' Belle said.

'I wouldn't blame him if he was angry forever. What I did was unforgivable.'

'You didn't make that decision alone. You both made it —you and Dad, for reasons that were appropriate at the time.' She couldn't deny how messy and raw it still felt, and maybe there was nothing to forgive or maybe there was everything, but she didn't have the strength or the will anymore to rage at past decisions.

'Whatever the case,' Grace said, 'just don't do what I did all those years ago. Don't leave anything to chance. Tell Andre you love him. Speak to him every day. And make plans for the future.'

Belle glanced out the window as they passed through St Leonards and the hospital where Edward had died, causing her to turn away from it. 'I think that ship has sailed, Mum.'

'What do you mean?'

'I'm fairly certain we're over.' She shook her head, her mind heavy and exhausted. 'The distance and the time difference. It's just become too hard. I'm not sure there's anything left for us.'

Grace patted her knee, her expression hopeful. 'There's always love.'

At her mother's house, Belle briefly visited her old room to gather any last belongings she'd left behind in her haste to leave for Scotland and met her mother again outside by her car.

'Thank you,' Grace said, drawing Belle's hair away from her eyes.

'For what?'

'For doing what I never had the courage to do. For finding Callum and telling him the truth.'

Belle shrugged. 'He kind of found me. And Hamish told him the truth.'

Grace laughed lightly. 'It doesn't matter. You went there and sought him out and that was incredibly brave of you.'

'I'm not trying to replace Dad,' she said, for it was important that her mother understood that. No matter how fraught or complex her relationship with Edward had been, he always was, and would always be, her father.

Grace nodded. 'I know. And if he was still alive, he would know that too.'

They embraced, Belle promising to return to visit on a free weekend, then she climbed into her car and drove home.

Peak hour had cleared, and the motorways were less cluttered, allowing for an easy drive back to Camden, which was just as well, for jetlag was dragging at her muscles and mind. It was with relief that she eventually turned onto Argyle Street, observing the line of jacarandas down the centre of the main thoroughfare. They'd been stark when she'd left, now they were a riot of purple spring flowers. The warm weather had brought people out too, and the side-walks were cluttered with folk—shops and cafés full. She thought of The Olive Grove and knew her first port of call would be to contact Carlo and let him know she was back, if she had any hope of keeping her job.

She turned into her driveway and cut the ignition, staring from the driver's seat at her small, three-bedroom house. The garden was becoming overgrown, weeds springing up to invade flowerbeds, and the warm sun had coaxed the grass from winter dormancy. It was almost guaranteed that a thick layer of dust coated every surface inside too and that she'd need to vacuum and open windows and do laundry.

Back to reality. Between work, the house, and the garden, she would throw herself into forgetting Andre. She would move on and focus only on what she could control. On what was in front of her. Anything more, she knew from experience, would simply sap her soul. And solace would come. Eventually. In layers and pieces and time. For time knew all—when to forgive, when to forget, when to breathe and heal again.

While she was sitting there, contemplating the next days and months, the front door of her house swung open, and someone stepped out onto her porch. She jumped as a familiar figure tossed a tea towel over one shoulder and leaned against the porch wall, smiling down at her.

Belle's heart hammered and she slowly opened the car door, climbing out and closing it again, walking towards the porch. She could only stare, flagging spirits lifting, light filling spaces where sorrow had set in.

'Andre.' Her voice was a whisper.

His smile broadened, his posture casual as he glanced at his watch. 'I thought you'd never get here.'

'What are you... but how?' She was lost for words, and she had to blink several times in case jetlag had caused hallucinations and the Andre on her porch was merely a mirage.

'You said in one of your voicemails that you were on your way back here. So I packed my bag and flew over too.'

'When did you get here?' She was still staring, unwilling to trust her eyes.

'Last night. Lucky you gave me a key.' He smiled again,

all bright eyes and white teeth and those irresistible, impossibly perfect dimples.

The key. Oh, thank the Lord she'd given him a key. And he'd used it, finding his way back to her.

She climbed the steps to the porch and when she reached him, she cupped his face in her hands, studying every line and curve—the day-old stubble, the brown eyes that were rich like hickory, the strand of hair that curled and fell over his eyes, tangling with his lashes.

She rose onto her toes and pressed her lips to his, her chest to his chest, his arms folding around her waist. She kissed him with all the uncertainty and anguish and worry she'd felt on the plane ride home, when she'd been sure it was over. And yet here he was, on her porch, his hands moving up her back and clenching her hair, eyes closed, moaning softly in her mouth. He was so real, so familiar, so close, and he kissed her like he had that very first time on the Corsia Agonale, and every time since then, as if it were the beginning again.

'If we're not careful, I'm going to have you right here on this step,' he murmured against her lips, voice thick with desire.

'I still can't believe you're here.' She pulled back, her eyes searching his desperately, breathing in the smell of his clean linen and cologne. 'I thought we were over. When I left all those messages and you didn't call me back, I thought that was it.'

'How can we be over when we haven't begun?' His gaze was serious and steady, holding hers, never looking away. 'I received your first message, then I wanted to surprise you. I told my father I was coming, arranged someone for the bar, then I packed my bag and flew here.'

'You flew here,' she repeated, still in disbelief.

'I hope you don't mind that I used the spare key to let myself in. I have meatballs on the stove, focaccia in the oven and Bellini in the fridge.'

Did she mind? She broke into a wide grin, her heart full. She kissed him again, a sweet ache growing in her thighs and moving up to her stomach, a hunger swelling inside her that wasn't for food. 'You surprise me every day,' she said. 'In the best possible way.'

He smiled, pleased with her compliment.

'How did your father react to you leaving?'

Andre's arms were still circled tightly around her. 'He was okay with it, surprisingly. I knew from the moment I left you in Fort William that I couldn't be without you. And he understood that. It's taken time, but now he knows.'

'How long are you here for?' she asked, already conscious of time, their ultimate nemesis.

'Three months, if you'll have me.'

'Three months?' The wonder and disbelief intensified. Of course she would have him—in her arms, in her bed. For every sleeping and waking moment, she would have him.

His arms left the circle of her waist and he draped one over her shoulder, drawing her in close. He dropped a kiss onto her head. 'So you found Callum?'

'We did,' Belle said. 'I have so much to tell you.'

'Then come, *signorina*. I want to hear all about it over an espresso.'

And just like that, they stepped into her house, into old ways and a familiar love. She had many homes now, places worthy of setting down roots—vibrant Sydney, colourful Rome and now, seaside Kirkcudbright. But she realised that home was also where Andre was, where they cooked and laughed and slept. Where they whispered to each other at night and held each other through the dawn. They'd been given another chance to remember the forgotten things, to learn new ones, to coax and memorise and explore again. Together. Wherever. Because love *was* enough.

ACKNOWLEDGMENTS

As always, my precious family were instrumental in making this book happen. Without their love and support, I could never afford the time to write, edit and publish my stories. Thank you, Brett, Eve and Connor for being patient, perfect and *you*!

Love and thanks to my cheer squad—Jo Libreri, Liz Butler, Natasha Booth, Bianca Nash and Erika Slaby. You are the perfect ingredient for any friendship, and I love you all dearly.

To my family, but particularly Carmen Montebello, and Joe and Michelle Montebello, thanks for the encouragement and endless moral support, and for talking about my books to anyone who will listen.

To my editors, Lynne Stringer and Marcia Batton, thank you once more for your extremely keen eyes. Special thanks to Marcia for your help with DNA and ancestry sites. It got this novel back on track when I noticed a major plot hole emerging.

To Kris Dallas, for your patience and another gorgeous cover, and to Tanya Nellestein and Rania Battany for being there to bounce ideas around with. And to Tanya for reading my manuscripts at the drop of a hat!

To my favourites in the industry, Helen Sibbritt, Craig and Phil from HappyValley BooksRead and Phillipa Nefri Clark, you are beautiful, kind, and brilliant at what you do. Thank you for being in my life.

And finally, to my incredibly loyal readers, none of this would be possible without you reading my books. I adore your messages, emails, and endless support, for it keeps me inspired and writing. Always stay in touch. You are part of this journey more than you know.

ALSO BY MICHELLE MONTEBELLO

www.michellemontebello.com.au

Seasons of Belle

The Summer of Everything

To Autumn, With Love

The Colour of Winter

The Spring Farewell

The Quarantine Station

The Lost Letters of Playfair Street

The Forever Place

Beautiful, Fragile

SEASONS OF BELLE - BOOK THREE

The Colour of Winter

MICHELLE MONTEBELLO

THE COLOUR OF WINTER
SEASONS OF BELLE: BOOK 3

After enduring a long-distance relationship for three years, Belle and Andre are finally reunited.

Blissfully married and living in Andre's Tuscan family home, they have their whole lives ahead of them. They're desperate to start a family and Belle is working to put the trauma of Paris behind her.

But when Christmas brings unexpected guests, Belle is caught off guard. Andre's ex-fiancée, Mary, her newborn baby, and her parents, are staying at the Tuscan house for the holidays.

Determined to make the best of a bad situation, Belle opens her arms and her home to them but is quickly undermined by Mary and her parents. The baby is a delight but is a constant reminder to everyone that Belle is yet to fall pregnant. And is it her imagination or is Andre spending more time with Mary and her baby?

Struggling with distrust, her inability to conceive and the ghosts of the past, Belle wonders if she'll make it through the holidays. And if the life she's always wanted with Andre will still be waiting for her at the end.

ABOUT THE AUTHOR

Michelle Montebello is a writer from Sydney, Australia where she lives with her family. She is the internationally bestselling author of *The Quarantine Station*, *The Forever Place* and *The Lost Letters of Playfair Street*.

Her books have won several awards. *The Quarantine Station* was a finalist in the 2021 International Book Awards for Best Historical Fiction. *The Lost Letters of Playfair Street* won the 2020 ARRA Awards for Favourite Contemporary Romance and Favourite Australian-Set Romance.

Michelle has been shortlisted twice for ARRA Australian Author of the Year.

If you would like to subscribe to her newsletter, visit www.michellemontebello.com.au.